THE GIRL IN THE BACKSEAT

OTHER BOOKS BY
NORMA CHARLES

Amanda Grows Up, Scholastic, 1978

No Place For A Horse, General, 1988

Un Poney Embarrassant, Les Edition Heritage, 1989

April Fool Heroes, Nelson, 1989

See You Later Alligator, Scholastic, 1991

À Bientôt, Croco!, Scholastic, 1991

Darlene's Shadow, General, 1991

Dolphin Alert! Nelson, 1998

Runaway, Coteau, 1999

Sophie Sea To Sea, Beach Holme, 1999

The Accomplice, Raincoast, 2001

Criss Cross, Double Cross, Beach Holme, 2002

Fuzzy Wuzzy, Coteau, 2002

All The Way to Mexico, Raincoast, 2003

Sophie's Friend in Need, Beach Holme, 2004

Boxcar Kid, Dundurn, 2007

The Girl in the Backseat

Norma Charles

RONSDALE PRESS

RONSDALE PRESS
3350 West 21st Avenue, Vancouver, B.C., Canada V6S 1G7
www.ronsdalepress.com

Typesetting: Julie Cochrane, in Minion 12 pt on 16
Front Cover Art: Janet Wilson
Cover Design: Julie Cochrane
Paper: Ancient Forest Friendly "Silva" — 100% post-consumer waste,
    totally chlorine-free and acid-free

Ronsdale Press wishes to thank the Canada Council for the Arts, the Government of Canada through the Book Publishing Industry Development Program (BPIDP), and the Province of British Columbia through the British Columbia Arts Council for their support of its publishing program.

Library and Archives Canada Cataloguing in Publication

Charles, Norma M.
    The girl in the backseat / Norma Charles.

ISBN 978-1-55380-056-9

    I. Title.

PS8555.H4224G57 2008   jC813'.54   C2007-907066-3

At Ronsdale Press we are committed to protecting the environment. To this end we are working with Markets Initiative (www.oldgrowthfree.com) and printers to phase out our use of paper produced from ancient forests. This book is one step towards that goal.

Printed in Canada by Marquis Printing, Quebec

For Jason, Melanie,
Andrea, Colin, and Michael,
and for Brian, of course,
who went on that memorable trip,
all the way to Winnipeg,
and beyond

ACKNOWLEDGEMENTS

Thank you, Jim (James Heneghan) for your many insightful suggestions with the manuscript.

And thank you, Linda Bailey, especially for the title.

Chapter one

"Ease out the clutch slowly while you give it more gas," Minerva Armstrong directed her brother. "Easy does it now . . ."

"Okay, okay, I got it." Jacob grunted, gripping the steering wheel.

He was concentrating so hard, beads of sweat popped out on his forehead and trickled down his face. He wiped his eye and pressed on the gas pedal. The red Mini Cooper lurched along the narrow driveway.

"More gas!" his sister yelled. "Give it more gas!"

The motor raced as they jolted forward.

"Watch out! Watch out!" Minerva grabbed the dashboard. "You'll crash into the house!"

Jacob gasped as the side of the house loomed up ahead of them. He swung the steering wheel left. Too far. The car crashed into the laurel hedge instead and came to an abrupt stop. He pitched forward, bashing his chin. The motor stalled.

"Now look what you made me do!" he yelled, clutching his throbbing chin.

"What *I* made you do?" his sister yelled back. "What do you mean? You're supposed to watch where you're going."

"Humph!" he huffed. "Some teacher!"

"That's it! I give up!" She shoved the door open. "You're hopeless. Worse than hopeless. No way in a million years will you ever learn to drive a car."

"So much for your teaching," he yelled after her. "You got to be the world's worst teacher."

Minerva slammed the car door so hard his ears popped. She stomped away into the house.

Jacob rubbed his aching chin and stared out at the shiny green leaves pressed against the windshield. His sweaty T-shirt stuck to the back of the leather seat. Now what? Bushes were jammed up against his door so he couldn't even get it open.

He clambered over the gear-shift to the passenger's seat and opened the other door. He thrashed his way into the bushes and tried to push the Mini out by leaning all his weight against the hood. The car was wedged so firmly in the hedge it wouldn't budge. No way could he get it out alone. No point asking his crabby sister for help.

He might as well get his soccer ball from the hall closet and get in a few good hard kicks against the garage door. Maybe it would help him think of something.

But as he tried to sneak past the kitchen door, his mother caught him.

"There you are, Jacob," she said. "That garbage needs emptying, my boy, and it's your turn. I shouldn't have to ask you every time."

His mom's hands were on her hips and her brown face was shiny with indignation. He could tell she was on a rampage about something. Probably with Minerva.

"Okay, okay." He wiped his sweaty face on his T-shirt and tried to yank the bag out of the garbage container. It was stuck so he had to kick it. He wanted to get out of that kitchen fast. He hated getting in the middle of the arguments his mom and Minerva were having these days.

"Now what's this?" his mother said to Minerva in a voice shrill with concern and heavy with her Jamaican accent. "You think I would allow a daughter of mine go right across the country to attend a school I haven't seen? In a city I haven't even visited? Where would you live, girl? Do they have safe dormitories at that university? No, no. I must go and see what this Winnipeg place is like for myself."

"Oh, Mom! I don't need you to come with me. I'm not a

little kid anymore, you know." Minerva was winding her curly hair into a twist. "I'm eighteen now."

Jacob knew his sister had planned to escape from their embarrassingly crazy family at the first opportunity. But now it looked as if her plans were dashed. Served her right for being so mean. He grunted as he gave the garbage bag another yank. It came out with a swoosh.

"Drive all the way to Winnipeg? What a marvelous idea, Rosa!" Fred Finkle said, hugging Jacob's mom. Fred Finkle was their step-father. He was a tall, bearded Englishman with a red nose and knobby knees. "Excellent! Excellent!" he said. "I can take my holidays in the last couple of weeks of August, and we'll all go, the whole family together, and see Minerva settled in her new school at the university in Winnipeg. We can camp and experience Western Canada's great prairie wilderness along the way. And visit our friends, Elizabeth and Roger, in the Kootenays. They're always inviting us, you know. And my brother's living in Brandon. We'll visit him and Peggy as well. We'll have a smashing time seeing the country. Banff, the Rockies, the Bad Lands, Drumheller where they have that world famous Dinosaur Museum . . . Why, I was told that . . ."

"Count me out," Jacob interrupted, relieved to have an excuse. "I've got soccer trials at the end of August. They're looking for players for the sixteen-and-under provincial team, and my coach said I have a good chance this year."

"Isn't that at the very end of August?" his mom asked

him. "Winnipeg is not that far away. We could be back in plenty of time for your trials."

"But I'd miss all the practices." Jacob was grasping at straws now.

"Practices!" she huffed. "Practising with that soccer ball is all you ever do, boy. You practise all day long. Every day. No, no. Fred's right. We will *all* go to Winnipeg. It will be fun. A good family holiday. That's what we need. A family that holidays together, stays together. Remember that wonderful trip a few years ago when we all drove down to Mexico? Now didn't we have fun?"

The kids all groaned. Even Barney and Sam groaned. Barney and Sam were Fred Finkle's sons and Jacob's stepbrothers. They were at the kitchen table playing a complicated version of The Lost World. Barney Finkle was a tall fourteen-year-old with spiky red hair and thick wirerimmed glasses. His brother, Sam Finkle, was eleven, and knew everything there was to know about dinosaurs.

The thought of that excruciating trip three years ago when all six of them had been squashed into a smelly old station wagon for a whole month while his mom and Fred had their honeymoon, made Jacob sweat even harder. The whole newly "blended" family had travelled all the way down the west coast from Vancouver to Mexico and back like some kind of crazy Brady bunch. A wonder they actually survived.

"What about visiting our mom?" Barney asked.

"She'll be out of the country until late September, son," Fred said. "Remember she's on assignment in South Africa?"

"Oh, right," Barney said.

Barney and Sam got to see their mom only on rare occasions when she was in town, between jobs. She was a wildlife photographer for *National Geographic*.

"Do we all have to go, Mom?" Jacob said, brushing sweat out of his eyes. "The van would be mega-crowded with the six of us and our camping gear, plus all Minerva's books and stuff. I could stay home and house-sit for you guys."

"I've got an idea," his mom said. "We can take two cars. We'll drive the van and, Minerva, you can drive the Mini. I was going to give it to you as a going-away gift anyway, now that Fred wants us to be a one-car family."

"Give me the Mini?" Minerva's scowl vanished and her face broke into a grin. "Sweet! I love that car!"

"So it's settled. I'll take the last two weeks in August off," Fred said. "Goldsmith Engineering Company will have to do without me." He checked the calendar on the wall above Jacob's head. "We'll leave on August fifteenth."

"But, but what about my try-outs . . ." Jacob squawked, ducking out of Fred's way.

"It takes less than a week to get to Winnipeg," Fred told him. "I reckon we could do it in three easy driving days if we had to. So as your mother said, we'll be back in plenty of time for your trials, Jacob, old chap. Don't get your bloomin' knickers in a knot, worrying about that."

Jacob stared gloomily at the calendar. He couldn't see any way of getting out of going on the trip. He knew his mom wouldn't allow him to stay home alone. No point even asking. You'd think she would, now that he was almost sixteen.

At least he and Minerva could get away from the rest of them in the Mini. He knew she'd let him ride with her. Maybe he'd even have a chance to drive it. He loved that peppy little Mini Cooper. It would be his last chance to learn to drive it until Minerva brought it home in the spring. And those roads on the flat prairie must be as straight as the centre line on a soccer field, so it would be a cinch to learn to drive there compared to their narrow twisting driveway. Maybe the family trip wouldn't be a total waste after all.

Now all he had to do was get that baby out of the hedge.

"Hey, guys," he said to Barney and Sam, as he dragged the bag of garbage to the back door. "Want to see something really cool outside?"

Chapter two

That night in another community several hundred kilometers east, Toby Avery pushed the back door open
silently and listened hard. Except for the chirping of night
insects, all was quiet.

She slipped out and felt her way along the grassy path.
She thought no one had followed her, but the night was so
dark she didn't know for sure. The grass was cool and damp
under her bare feet. She squeezed the flashlight in her pocket but didn't dare turn it on yet. She couldn't wait to get
back to her book. It was hidden behind the shed they used
for a chicken coop.

She knew from the smell that the shed was near. She ducked into the bushes and picked her way through the blackberry vines, her arms up to protect her face from thorns.

A noise! She froze and listened hard. A fluttering mumble. She smiled. It was just the hens inside the chicken coop, clucking and fluffing up their feathers, settling for the night.

She pushed through the thorny vines to the back of the shed. She reached under the building, lifted a flat rock and felt around in the dry powdery dirt for the smooth texture of the plastic bag. There it was. Inside the bag was a book that seemed to pulse with excitement and energy when she touched it. *The Adventures of Mighty Mavis*. Flicking on her tiny flashlight, she opened the book where she had left off a few nights ago and caught her breath in anticipation.

A girl and her brother were hunting for their little sister who had become lost at the beach on a family picnic.

"There she is!" the girl cried out and ran forward in the sand. But it wasn't their little sister after all. It was . . .

Then Toby heard her own name. She switched off her light and bit her lip.

"Tobia? Tobia? Are you out here? It is much past bedtime now."

It was Bertha, her father's newest wife. Although Bertha was just a couple of years older than Toby and her three half-brothers, she took her duties as the newest step-mother of all Toby's father's children very seriously, finding fault in everything they did. Behind her back, they called her "Big Bad Bertha" or "Big B.B." for short.

"Tobia Elizabeth!" Bertha called again. "I know you are out here."

In the darkness, the chickens clucked and grumbled back at her.

Bertha slashed at the grass and blackberry vines near the chicken pen, flashing her powerful light around the bushes. Toby crouched low behind the shed and held her breath.

Bertha stomped closer and closer, slashing and muttering. "Where is that girl . . ."

Toby wrapped her arms over her head, willing herself to become invisible.

"Aha! So that is where you're hiding!" Bertha shouted, flashing her light into Toby's eyes, blinding her.

Before Toby could escape, Bertha grabbed the back of her nightdress and yanked her upright. Toby fumbled to hide the book behind a bush, but she was too late.

"A book!" The big girl swooped down and grabbed it. Her breath reeked of stale onions and anger. "Sneaking around reading this filthy book, are you? The devil's words! You just wait until your father hears about this!"

Toby lunged away, but the bigger girl's grasp on her nightdress was far too strong. "Please don't tell him," Toby begged, her voice cracking. "Oh, please, please don't tell Father."

"The wicked must be punished," Bertha grunted as she

hauled Toby to her feet. "It is for your own good, you know. You do not wish to be cast out into the Darkness and burn in Hell's Inferno forever for all eternity, do you?"

Blackberry thorns tore at Toby's arms and face and legs as Bertha shoved her forward through the bushes. Toby flinched and stumbled, but Bertha held her firmly by her nightdress.

Toby knew there was no point trying to get away. Not from Bertha; she was too strong. And not from her father's wrath. He would beat her for sure.

Toby felt her heart shrink. She wished she were dead.

Chapter three

"If you have any problems, contact us with your walkie-talkie," Jacob's mom told him and Minerva as she got into the family van, a dark blue Villager, a few weeks later. It was mid-August and a sunny day for the start of the Finkle-Armstrong journey to Winnipeg to take Minerva to the University of Manitoba.

"First stop except for gas and a picnic lunch at Manning Park will be our friends, Patrick and Joan's place in the Kootenays," Fred said. "They told me they had plenty of room for us to camp in their yard tonight."

"And you can bet the price will be right," Jacob muttered

to Minerva as he stuffed his backpack and soccer ball into the Mini and slammed his door shut.

"Frugal Fred Finkle strikes again." She grinned at her brother. Fred was famous for his penny-pinching ways.

As Minerva backed the Mini down the driveway, Jacob shifted in the front seat, trying to get comfortable. He threaded his feet around his pack and bounced his soccer ball on his knee. "Sure is crowded in here," he muttered.

"Put your pack in the back," she said. "Plenty of room back there."

"With all your stuff? No way. I'd never see it again."

"Ah, quit your complaining," she said. "How about some music?"

Jacob flipped through their CDs and came up with a Graft album, which he slid into the CD player and turned up the volume. High energy music poured out as Minerva turned the car down the road to follow the van in which the rest of the family was travelling. The yellow kayak strapped to the roof rack made it easy to keep the van in sight in the traffic.

She opened her window wide and a fresh breeze blew in. "That's better," she said, tapping the steering wheel in time with the music.

"At least we can play our own music as loud as we want," Jacob said.

As they went east from Vancouver along the highway just north of the Canada–US border, he watched how Minerva was driving, how when they had to slow down, she changed gears by pressing down on the clutch and moving the gear lever.

"That changing gears is the trickiest part, but I bet I could do it," Jacob told her. "I could drive this baby. How about giving me a chance?"

"And we end up in some hedge again? No thanks."

"Our driveway is so narrow and twisty you have to be an expert not to end up in the hedge. Come on. I know I could do it."

"Okay, okay. But not here. Too much traffic. Let's wait until we get to the prairies. The roads will probably be quieter and straighter."

"Promise you'll let me take the wheel then? It'll be my last chance to drive this baby for a whole year."

"All right. I promise. I promise."

Minerva drove on to Manning Park where they stopped for a picnic lunch with the rest of the family, then they continued for another four hundred kilometers, toward their first stop for the night in the Kootenays in south-eastern BC, always keeping the family van, alias the Max, in sight up ahead.

About six hours later, they turned off the highway to a gravel road that led eventually to their friend's farm beside a narrow river. Before the turnoff to the friend's place, Jacob saw a sign made with white pebbles on the grassy knoll beside the neighbour's dirt driveway. "REPENT THE END IS NEAR."

"What does that mean?" Jacob wondered. "The end of what?"

"Probably the end of the world," Minerva said. "Some religious people are always predicting that the end of the world will happen anytime now. They say you better be good and pray hard or you won't be saved, and you'll have to burn in hell forever. At least that's what some people believe."

Jacob raised his eyebrows and grunted. "Yeah, right."

Patrick and Joan welcomed the family and showed them where to set up their tents in their grassy backyard. Their daughter Claire was going into grade twelve in September and she wanted to hear how Minerva managed to get into a university in Manitoba, something she wanted to do herself.

"Want to come and see the new workshop?" Patrick invited them. "We're just putting the finishing touches on it."

"Love to," Fred said. "I'm curious. How did you raise those huge beams up for the ceiling? Block and tackle?"

Patrick started a long complicated description of how the workshop was built.

Jacob yawned. Boring! He tossed his soccer ball to Barney Finkle and Barney tossed it back. Jacob escaped to the field behind the workshop and Barney followed him. Jacob used every chance he got to practise his dribbling and kicking. Or to try and improve the Finkle brothers' soccer skills, which was a lost cause if there ever was one. It was a toss up who was clumsier: Barney, or his younger brother, Sam.

As Jacob and Barney kicked the soccer ball back and forth, Barney tried out some horse jokes and riddles. His jokes were never that good, but these were especially bad.

"Why did the horse go over the mountain?" he asked Jacob.

Jacob smothered another yawn, and nudged the ball to Barney. "Don't know. Why?"

Barney missed the ball so he had to chase it close to a fence made with spindly poles. "Because he couldn't go under it," he yelled back to Jacob. "Get it? Go *under* the mountain."

"Right. Right. Now that's got to be one of the worst jokes I've ever heard. It's not even a joke. It's a riddle. Why don't you just give up?"

"What?" Barney shoved up his glasses and kicked the ball back to Jacob. "Give up my dream of being a world-famous stand-up comedian? You know how much money those guys make? I want to be rich."

"You got to admit that horses just aren't all that funny. Not even as funny as cows. Why don't you think of something else to make jokes about?" Jacob trapped the ball, dribbled it and made a swift pass back to Barney. Of course Barney missed it. He ran after it clumsily, tripping over his own long feet.

When Jacob finally got the ball back, he said, "Okay, Barn. This is important. Concentrate on the ball. Say I'm in goal. Try to get the ball past me. Now give it all you got." He waved his arms at Barney.

Barney stepped back and gave the ball a mighty kick. It flew way over Jacob's head and sailed into the yard next door.

"You didn't have to kick it that hard," Jacob grumbled, climbing the fence after it.

"Sorry. But you did say to give it all I had." Barney followed Jacob into the neighbour's yard.

On the other side of the bushes, a bunch of kids were playing around on a grassy field. They wore old-fashioned clothes, dresses with long skirts for the girls, and long-sleeved shirts and pants held up with braces for the boys. The smallest kids stopped shrieking and tearing around. They stared openly at Jacob, as if they had never seen a brown person up close before.

"Your hair looks funny," one little boy with long blond hair piped up in a squeaky voice, pointing at Jacob.

Jacob grinned at the kid and shook his "dreadlocks" at him. They were so long now that he could shake them over his eyes.

The kid and his friend giggled.

One of the girls, an older one wearing a pink dress with a long skirt and long sleeves, came over to Jacob.

"Where are you from?" she asked. She had blond hair in a braid down her back and her face and hands were covered with angry red scratches as if she had been in a fight with a vicious cat.

"Vancouver," Jacob told her.

"We're on our way to Winnipeg," Barney said. "Hey, you guys ever hear the one about why the horse went over the mountain?"

The girl frowned. "What horse? You have a horse?" she asked with concern.

"Because it couldn't get under it?" Barney said.

The kids stared at him blankly.

"You know." He waved his arms around. "The horse had to go *over* the mountain, because he couldn't get *under* the mountain. Get it? It's a joke."

"A riddle," Jacob said.

"Oh. A joke. A riddle." The girl nodded. Her bright smile made Jacob forget the scratches on her face. "Did you boys say you were going to Winnipeg?"

Jacob nodded.

"How are you getting there?"

"We're driving," Barney said. "All the way to Winnipeg, camping all the way." He made it sound like a song.

"We've got two cars," Jacob told her. "That blue van over there, and my sister's driving the red Mini." He pointed through the bushes to the two vehicles parked on the other side of the fence.

A gong sounded and the kids rushed off without saying good-bye. The girl in the pink dress ran away too, but she stopped to stare back at Jacob and Barney. For a second it looked as if she were about to ask them something else, but she changed her mind and turned away to follow the others.

Chapter four

T he next morning was another sunny day. They broke
camp early. Jacob packed up his tent and stuffed it into
the Mini's hatchback. Then after many thanks and invita-
tions to Patrick, Joan and Claire to come and visit them in
Vancouver, they were on the road before nine o'clock. They
were heading north now, through the mountains, toward
Radium Hot Springs on the western edge of Banff National
Park, Minerva and Jacob in the Mini following the rest of
the family in the Max.

Jacob shoved his pack and his ball down under his legs
and propped his feet up on the Mini's dashboard. He hated
being so crowded. "Sure not much room in here. Feels like

being in a stuffed sausage," he muttered.

"Are you going to moan and complain the whole trip?" Minerva snapped. "Because if you are, you can shift your gear into the van and ride there instead."

"Okay, okay," Jacob said, yawning. "Don't know how many of Barney's horse jokes and riddles I can take. At least we can have our own music here."

"Right. How about playing that new Jill Salvadore CD?"

Jacob flipped through the box of CDs to hunt for his sister's request. He slid it into the player and peppy music blasted out.

Before they had gone far, Minerva said, "What's that noise?"

"What noise? I didn't hear anything. Just the music."

"I think I heard something from the backseat."

Out of the corner of his eye, Jacob noticed a movement behind him. He swung around and stared at the purple quilt Minerva had spread over her stuff. The lump under it looked different somehow. He lifted the edge of the quilt.

"Holy Toledo!" he shouted.

"What?" Minerva slammed on the brakes and the car swerved to the road's edge.

"There's a girl back there!"

Grabbing the quilt, the girl stared back at them, her eyes huge with fear. "Please," she pleaded in a scared voice. "Oh please, don't stop. Sorry, sorry, but I just have to get away. You're my only chance. You've got to help me!"

"Get away? From where? Why?" Minerva asked, steering the Mini back onto the road. "Who are you? What are you doing in our car?"

Jacob lowered the music's volume. "Aren't you the girl with those kids we were talking to yesterday?"

She was still wearing the frilly pink dress with long sleeves and her face and hands were covered with scratches.

The girl swallowed and nodded. "When you said you were going to Winnipeg, I thought this would be my only chance to esca . . . to . . . to get to my aunt's place. She lives in Winnipeg."

"So why don't you take the bus?" Jacob asked. "You know what, Min? We should stop and let this kid out. We can't take her all the way to Winnipeg. We're already crowded."

"Oh, please," the girl begged. "Please, don't stop the car. I really, really need a ride. There's no way they would let me go."

"Who wouldn't let you?"

"My father and the other elders. You are my only hope." There was a note of desperation in her voice that made Jacob listen.

"So why do you need to leave? Why do you want to go to your aunt's place?" Minerva asked her. "Why don't you just stay home? Why do you have to run away? What could be so bad? What's the big deal?"

The girl stared out the window and blinked hard. She sniffed and rubbed her nose on the back of her hand. Finally she said, "Next month in September is my birthday. I will be turning fourteen. And my father, well, they caught me, and he's arranged . . ." She stopped as if she couldn't go on. She swallowed hard.

"Caught you doing what?" Jacob wanted to know.

"I was reading a book."

"Reading is forbidden? That's crazy," Jacob said. "What's this awful thing that's going to happen to you?"

"Something so awful." The girl shut her eyes and shuddered.

He waited for an explanation, but she just shook her head.

"What could be that bad?" he asked.

She stared at him. "After I got caught . . ." she said hesitantly. Tears flooded her eyes and a sob caught at her throat. She hid her face behind her hands.

"If it's really that bad, you should go to the police," he said. "You could call the children's help line, or something."

The girl didn't answer.

"You should just go to the police," Jacob repeated. "They'd help if you're in some kind of trouble."

The girl wiped her tears on her sleeve and cleared her throat. "The police?" she said in a wobbly voice. "No. Another girl, my friend, Leslie, tried that last year. She ran away to town and went to the police."

"Good for her."

"But, but . . . they just brought her back to her parents. Said she was a runaway."

"Then what happened?"

"The elders had a big secret meeting and decided to send her off right away."

"Send her off? Where?"

"To the States somewhere. I don't know where exactly. But we never heard from her again." The girl shook her head. "No letters. Nothing. She just disappeared."

"We should tell Mom," Jacob said. "She'd know what to do."

"No! Oh, please, please don't tell anyone I'm here," the girl begged. She was frantic. "Especially not your parents. They would say I was a runaway too, like Leslie, and send me back to my parents. They would say that is where I belong. And then, and then . . ."

"I've never heard of such a thing. Have you?" Jacob asked Minerva.

Minerva shrugged and was about to say something when a grey van overtook them.

The girl squealed and ducked, pulling the quilt over her head.

"What?" Jacob said. "Who's in that van?"

The girl peeked out from under the quilt at the van ahead of them. She pushed the quilt away from her face. "That one's not from the commune. But for sure, my father will be coming after me. If he catches me before I get to my aunt's place in Winnipeg, he'll force me to go back home. And then, and then. . . ."

"What about your mother?" Minerva asked. "Can't you talk to her?"

"She always agrees with my father."

"Our mom's really nice and understanding about most things. She'd know what to do to help you."

Toby shook her head. "If you tell her, she'll have to tell your father. And then they'd call the police. That's what always happens."

"Fred's not really our dad. He's our step-father," Jacob said. "Our dad died in a car accident a few years ago. Then after a while, Mom married Fred."

A picture of Jacob's dad flashed into his head. A tall man with a big grin, who loved soccer as much as Jacob did. Their Saturdays were always totally devoted to soccer. He'd take Jacob to his weekly soccer game at least half an hour early to "get in some good kicks," as he called it. Then they'd spend the rest of the day catching all the MLS and English Premiership games on TV.

Jacob picked up his soccer ball from the floor, hugged it close and rested his chin on it. Even after all this time, sometimes the longing for his dad was overwhelming.

"I'd feel better if you didn't tell anyone at all about me," Toby said. She sounded calmer now. "Just let me stay here in the back of the car until we get to Winnipeg. That's all I ask."

"What's your name?" Minerva asked her.

"Toby."

"I'm Minerva, and my brother is Jacob."

The girl nodded. "So, can I stay? I won't be any trouble at

all. You don't have to do anything special. I'll just hide back here and I won't be in your way. Winnipeg is not so far away. We should be there in a couple of days. Right?"

"Couple of days!" Minerva snorted. "Dream on. That would be if we were going straight there. But I can tell you from past experience that travelling with Fred and our mom, we have to stop to see all the sights and inspect every little thing along the way. Fred said we could get there in three days, but we'll be lucky to be there in a week, I bet." She glanced over to Jacob with a question in her eyes: what should they do?

He shrugged back at her. It bothered him that the girl was so insistent they not tell anyone. He didn't like keeping secrets from his mom. When she found out, as she usually did, he always got into big trouble.

The road north through the heavily forested mountains was quiet, so they passed only the occasional vehicle. Every time a vehicle drew near, Toby ducked under Minerva's quilt until it had sped past.

Eventually, as they were driving along a broad valley following a meandering river, surrounded by mountain cliffs, their walkie-talkie beeped.

Jacob picked it up. "Mini here," he said.

"We'll be in Radium soon," his mom's voice came in, over the crackles. "We're stopping for gas at the first place we see."

"Sounds good," Jacob said.

When they arrived at the village of Radium, a small collection of motels, gift shops and restaurants on both sides of the highway, the van stopped at a gas station. Minerva drove the Mini up beside it. Toby ducked under the quilt.

"We're thinking of having a break after we've gassed up," Jacob's mom told them through her open window. "Fancy a dip in the hot springs? According to my map, they're just east of the village."

"Sounds great," Minerva said. "I could use a break. We'll follow you after we gas up."

A few minutes later, Minerva found a vacant spot for the Mini under some trees in a parking lot beside a big aquatic centre that had been built into the rocks. "The shade will keep you a bit cooler," she said to Toby.

Jacob rummaged through his pack for his bathing suit and towel. Toby had already ducked under the quilt. He was going to tell her that she should come in for a swim too, but he knew she wouldn't. "See you later," he said.

On their way to the pools, he said to Minerva, "I still think we should tell Mom about Toby. She'd know what to do."

"Let's wait a bit," Minerva whispered. "Toby really doesn't want us to."

"But we're helping her run away from home."

"I know, but I'm sure she has her reasons. And they must be really important reasons. Didn't you notice all her scratches and bruises? Someone's obviously been beating her. If we do tell Mom, she'd probably tell Fred. And there's no telling what he'll do. He might contact the police and . . ."

Their mom joined them. "So how's the driving, Min?"

Minerva shot a warning look at Jacob, so he clammed up. "Good," she said. "Beautiful scenery."

"Are you comfortable driving in the mountains? I could take over for a while if you like."

"Oh, I'm loving it," Minerva assured her.

"Let me know when you want a break."

"I will."

Chapter five

Toby crouched on the floor in the narrow space between the leather backs of the front seats and the backseat. She shifted uncomfortably. Her lower back ached especially where her father had whipped her a few days ago, and the floor was hard, but if she moved up onto the backseat, she'd have to cover herself with the quilt and that would be too hot. She searched under the quilt and found a yellow cushion with a smiley face on it. She sat on that and was a little more comfortable.

At her feet was a bundle of plastic bottles containing a clear liquid. She worked one bottle out of the bundle.

"Aegean Springs. Pure life. Natural Spring water," the label declared. That was something new. Water in a plastic bottle? She had never seen that before. She unscrewed the lid and took a small sip. Tasted like regular water. She gulped down half the bottle. She had not realized how thirsty she was. The water was good and blessedly refreshing.

She leaned back and stared up out of the side window. All she could see was a leafy branch against a pale blue sky with a few puffy clouds drifting slowly across the window. Must be afternoon now. Everyone in the commune would know she was missing. Her father's face would be purple with rage. He'd blame her mother for her disappearance. She knew that, although her mother had nothing at all to do with it. Her father would probably call an emergency meeting of the elders, and they'd set out on a search with the pack of fierce hunting dogs. They'd send out word to all the other Brethren in the surrounding area and soon everyone would be out searching for her.

A green pickup truck backed up beside the Mini and slid across Toby's view of the sky, blocking it. She pulled the quilt over her head and caught her breath. Doors clunked open and a noisy family climbed out. She couldn't see them but she could hear their loud voices, adults and children. A woman said, "Now don't forget your towels, girls." And a girl's voice said, "Has anyone seen my brush?" Doors slammed shut followed by high-pitched barking. They had left a dog behind in the pickup.

Toby peeked out from behind the quilt. It was a thin whippet-looking dog with a long narrow nose and dark brown eyes. It stared out the truck window into the Mini right at Toby and barked again.

The Brethren were everywhere. Maybe even that jolly family were members. Although she had never seen a dog like this one in any of the Brethren families, she'd better not take any chances.

She pulled the quilt over her head again. It was dim under the quilt, and stuffy. Toby leaned back and closed her eyes. If only she could be in Winnipeg right now where she would be safe. When were Minerva and her brother ever coming back?

🚗 🚗 🚗

Jacob lowered himself into the warm water and felt the dust and tiredness from the road wash away. While Minerva and his mom lounged in the huge shallow steamy pool of the hot springs, he had followed the Finkles to splash around in the cooler pool and to do some laps. It was a relief not to have to think about their stowaway for awhile.

After they'd finished their swim and had showered and changed into regular clothes, they met in the lobby where they loaded up on snacks from the vending machines.

"Why can't they sell some good healthy food at these places?" Jacob's mom complained, watching Minerva carrying a couple of cans of pop and bags of taco chips out of the lobby.

Jacob almost blurted out to his mom about Toby, but he remembered how firm both she and Minerva had been that no one else know she was hiding in the Mini. Instead, he asked, "Where are we spending the night tonight?"

"There's excellent camping in Banff National Park," Fred said. "We'll drive on until we find a vacancy in one of the camp grounds."

"Would you like to ride in the van for awhile?" Jacob's mom asked Jacob. "Give you a break?"

"Oh no," Jacob said, quickly. "I like the Mini. We can play our CDs as loud as we want."

As they continued east along the highway through a narrow gap in the mountains and into Banff Park, Toby munched happily on the taco chips and gulped down the pop. "Yum," she said, devouring the chips. "So delicious! What are these called?"

"Just plain taco chips," Minerva said. "Haven't you had them before?"

"No. I did have potato chips once though, but that was a long time ago when I was a little kid."

"What about when you go to town? Don't you ever buy a snack then?"

"We don't go to town very often. I can't remember the last time. By the way, I drank one of those bottles of Aegean Spring water. I hope you don't mind."

"That's okay," Minerva said. "So what grade are you in? Where do you go to school?" She fired questions at the girl.

"There's a school right on our commune where the little kids go, but I finished a couple of years ago."

"You're finished school already?"

"Our school goes to just grade six."

"What about high school?"

Toby shrugged and stared out the window.

"If you don't go to school, what do you usually do all day?"

"There's always plenty of work looking after the little kids and feeding the chickens and gathering eggs, and helping in the garden too. I like that the best. I even learnt how to drive the tractor last summer. One of my brothers taught me."

"You're so lucky to have a brother to teach you to drive," Jacob said, looking at Minerva meaningfully.

She ignored him and asked Toby, "How many brothers do you have? And sisters?"

"Well, my mom has five children. Two boys, two girls and me. I'm the oldest of the girls. But counting all my half-brothers and sisters, there are forty-eight of us children, all together."

"Forty-eight!" Minerva squealed. "All in one family!" The car swerved to the road's shoulder and gravel sprayed up under the wheel-well. "Holy man!"

Jacob grabbed the dashboard, but Minerva turned the wheel to steer back onto the blacktop. "Wow!" he said. "I never knew you could have that many kids in one family."

"Ours isn't the biggest family in the commune. Not yet anyway."

"Families even bigger than that?" Jacob said. "Sounds impossible."

"Do you all live in the same house?" Minerva asked.

"One huge house. Us girls have the whole attic, and the boys sleep in the basement, and everyone else is on the main floor. And that's where we eat too."

"Everyone else?"

"My mother, and all her sister-wives. And the babies of course."

"Sister-wives?" Minerva asked. "What's a sister-wife? I don't think I've heard of sister-wives."

"It's all my father's wives. He just got his fourteenth."

"Oh!" Minerva's eyebrows shot up. "Where we live, a man can have only one wife at a time."

"But how else can he get into heaven?"

"What do you mean?"

"The Good Book says that if you want to be saved, you have to have more than one wife. And the more wives and children you have, the more glorified you will become when you reach paradise."

"I've never heard of that."

"It's true."

Jacob asked, "How do you know it's true?"

"Because the prophet says it's true."

"And you believe it, just because some guy says so?"

"It's not just any guy," Toby said. "It's the prophet."

"Okay," he shrugged. "If that's what you want to believe, go right ahead. But it sure sounds weird to me. One man with fourteen wives and forty-eight children? Mega-weird."

They camped in Gold Stream Campground in the park. The campground was in a lightly forested area near a small bubbling river. Nice but there was nowhere level for Jacob to kick his ball around except on the narrow beach.

"Can you give me a hand with the boat?" Fred asked him.

Jacob helped Fred unload the yellow kayak from the roof rack and carry it to the water's edge. Fred climbed in and paddled away into the fast-flowing stream, skillfully avoiding the rocks. He paddled upstream to a pool where he did several expert Eskimo rolls, flipping the boat over and bobbing back upright. Neat, Jacob thought as he kicked his ball against a big square rock. The guy sure could handle that boat. He's a real pro. Wonder where he learned to kayak so well.

Supper was ready soon. Roti with curried beans and rice. One of Jacob's favourites. Since he was on dishwashing, he managed to sneak Toby a bowl of leftover beans and rice as well as some cookies. He still thought they should tell their mom about her, but meanwhile, they couldn't let her starve.

"Sure you'll be okay back there?" he asked her as she settled with the food under the quilt in the backseat. "Looks awfully cramped to me."

"It's lovely," Toby said. "Cozy. And safe."

Chapter six

The next morning as they drove through Banff National Park after an early breakfast, Jacob stared out the Mini window at the jagged rocky mountain peaks and lakes bluer than blue. They were heading north on the eastern side of the Rocky Mountains.

"Wow! Those mountains sure are something else," he said.

"Highest ones I've ever seen," Toby piped up from the backseat.

"How did you sleep?" Minerva asked her.

"Once I got to sleep it was fine," she said. She was peeling an orange Minerva had saved her from breakfast and the tangy smell of orange peel filled the car. "Don't worry about me."

Jacob put on a Lobear CD and reggae music poured out of the speakers. He tapped his fingernails on the dashboard in time with the catchy beat.

"I like that music," Toby said. "Makes me feel like dancing."

"Makes me feel like that too," Minerva said. "You ever heard of the West Edmonton Mall?"

"No. I know that Edmonton is the capital of Alberta. That's all I know about it. I've never been there. Have you?"

"No. The mall's supposedly one of the biggest in Canada and they're probably having fantastic sales now, so my mother and I want to go shopping there for some winter clothes for school. That's where we're heading today."

"Mall shopping!" Jacob groaned. "Mega-boring! Can't think of anything I hate more."

After driving for hours due north, always keeping the van in sight, they arrived in Edmonton. Near the entrance of the huge mall, Minerva found a parking spot for the Mini beside some shrubs.

"You sure you'll be all right here in the car?" she asked Toby.

"I'll be fine. Don't worry about me."

"We might be a while."

"That's okay. I can just wait."

"Maybe I'll wait here too," Jacob said.

"You can't, Jay," Minerva said. "Mom and Fred would come over and they might find Toby."

"Which may not be such a bad thing, as far as I'm concerned."

"Don't be like that. Maybe Mom will buy you a new T-shirt or something."

"A new T-shirt. Whippee ding, ding!"

But Jacob followed Minerva inside where they met the Finkles and their mom studying the big map of the mall.

Fred said, "Let's have a plan. I'm sure you ladies don't want us trailing along while you shop. So maybe the boys and I could go to the aquatic centre. I read in my guide book that this mall has one of the biggest wave pools and highest slides in Western Canada."

"Sounds fun," Barney said.

Even Sam looked enthusiastic.

Jacob was torn. He sure didn't like the idea of following his mom and sister around ladies' clothing shops like a little puppy dog. On the other hand, he knew from past experience that spending an afternoon with Fred and his boys could be awfully painful.

"We'll shop for just a while, then we'll join you for a dip in the pool," Jacob's mom said. "How about that?"

Jacob finally opted to go with Fred.

At the aquatic centre's entrance, Jacob's mom and Minerva stood in line with them to find out what the hours of the pool were so they could join them later.

"What! It costs that much just for a couple of bloomin'

hours of swimming?" frugal Fred protested to the cashier.

Other people standing in the line behind them tittered. Jacob felt his face flush red with embarrassment.

"Sorry, sir, but those are our summer rates," the cashier said. Jacob was sure she was trying not to laugh in Fred's face. "We do have a family rate that works out a bit less."

"The family rate then." Fred grudgingly opened his wallet. "My wife and, um, daughter will be joining us later, but I'll get them a ticket now. Will that be a problem?"

"No, sir. But the family rate is for just *one* family." She looked pointedly at Minerva and Jacob's brown skin and curly hair. Jacob knew she was wondering how they could fit into this tall, slim English family. It was something he often wondered himself.

Fred got huffy. "I assure you, Miss, that this boy is part of my family. As well as this woman and her daughter. What do you want? A bloomin' marriage certificate?" His voice rose. The line behind them fell silent.

Jacob wished there was a rock he could crawl under and disappear.

"That's quite all right, sir," the woman said quickly. "Here's your family pass. Have a good swim. Next customer, please."

Jacob rushed inside, trying to distance himself from the embarrassing situation.

As soon as he got his bathing suit on, he ran out and jumped into the pool. As the cool water splashed over his head, he forgot about his embarrassment and even about their stowaway for the moment.

The pool was fantastic with waves big enough to surf in, even bigger than those at Jericho Beach in Vancouver.

"Come on, Jay! Race you to the top!" Barney yelled.

"You're on!" Jacob yelled back and they raced up the stairs of the highest slide, six storeys high. He didn't overtake Barney until they reached the top. By that time, they were both breathless. Jacob took a deep breath then flung himself down the slide. After a couple of seconds of weightless falling, there was a moment of scary darkness as he swished through a tunnel. At the bottom he catapulted into the water. Barney bobbed up right behind him.

"So cool!" Barney yelled. "Want to go again?"

"All right!"

An hour or so after his mom and Minerva had joined them, Jacob felt so sodden he suspected that he was dissolving into the warm water.

Minerva said, "Think I'll head back to the car now."

"I'm ready to leave too," Jacob said.

"What? So soon?" Fred said. "We should at least get our full money's worth. We can't leave yet."

Minerva frowned. Jacob knew she was worried about Toby.

The sun was low on the horizon when they finally left the mall, dragging their waterlogged feet into the parking lot.

Chapter seven

After Minerva and Jacob went into the shopping mall,
Toby peeked out at the dusty grey shrubs in front of
the car. The glaring afternoon sun beat directly on the car
roof and it soon grew stifling hot and airless. They had left
the front windows open a few centimeters, but it was still
way too stuffy. What she would give for a breath of fresh air
and a drink of good cool water! They'd finished all the
Aegean Spring water.

Also, she needed to use the washroom, desperately. With
all those shoppers, there must be a public washroom in the
mall. Should she chance sneaking in? Minerva said they

would not be back for awhile. She didn't dare leave the car dressed in her frilly pink dress. People would notice her right away.

She had only a change of underwear and her toothbrush in her own small backpack, but beside her on the backseat was Minerva's pack. Toby rummaged through it and pulled out a pair of dark blue shorts and a plain black T-shirt. She quickly shook off her dress and pulled on the T-shirt over her vest. Her second layer of long white underwear pants went down to her ankles and they would show if she wore the shorts. So she pulled them off too, and slipped on the shorts. They were big, but they had a draw-string waist which she could tighten so they wouldn't fall down.

Her pale bare legs looked like stuffed sausages. She quickly averted her eyes from them. The only time she ever saw her legs was when she had a shower or changed her long underwear once a week. The laws in the commune stated that girls must always appear fully clothed, and that included covering their legs and arms. Even when they went swimming in the pond, they wore long-sleeved bathing-dresses that covered their knees.

Now her hair. Jacob had left his blue Brazil cap on the dash. She climbed into the front seat. As she reached for the cap, she happened to glance into the rearview mirror. Parked in the next row of vehicles was a beige van with darkened windows and a roof rack.

Her father's van!

She gasped and ducked down.

Her heart raced.

It couldn't be his van, she told herself. It just couldn't! There was no way he could have followed her here, all the way to Edmonton. How would he know she was travelling in the Mini? She trembled at the thought that maybe it *was* him, and he was just sitting in there, waiting for a chance to grab her.

She slowly raised her head and peeked into the rearview mirror again. She couldn't see any movement in the van. But with its darkened windows it was hard to tell if anyone was in there.

She really had to go to the washroom now. She wriggled on the seat uncomfortably. She would have to chance it.

She stuffed her braid into Jacob's cap and settled it securely on her head. Then she cautiously opened the car door and slipped out. Staring straight ahead, she hurried across the pavement and into the mall, ducking into the crowd of shoppers. She glanced around. She didn't think anyone had followed her.

It didn't take long to find the women's washroom. She pushed the door open. The washroom was all shiny tiles and chrome with a row of sinks and another row of toilets in cubicles. She'd never seen so many sinks. Or so many toilets. Or so much shininess.

She drew in a deep breath. Everything smelled clean and fresh.

She ducked into one of the cubicles and used the toilet. What a relief!

She left the cubicle and stood in front of a sink. She pulled off Jacob's cap and turned on the tap, splashing cool water on her burning face and neck. A huge mirror stretched across the whole wall in front of her. A small blond girl with scratched pink cheeks and wearing an over-sized black T-shirt stared back at her with serious blue eyes. It took a second to realize it was herself.

"Hot day, eh?" A fat woman beside her was patting her sweating face and arms with a paper towel.

"Very hot," Toby said, grabbing the hat. She nipped back into the cubicle and locked the door. She sat down and looked around. This was one place where no one could follow her.

After a few minutes, she had cooled down. She felt naked without her long underwear and skirt. She pulled the T-shirt and shorts down as far as they would go to cover her pale legs and left the washroom, slipping into the crowd of shoppers again. There weren't as many now. Each shop along the broad corridor had big windows with colourful displays. She stood in front of one shop window filled with pretend people dressed in the skimpiest of clothes, just a few bits of brightly coloured cloth. My, my! How could women dress like that? Maybe this is what the prophet was talking about when he said the cities were filled with sinners clad in scanty garments.

She pulled Minerva's shorts further down over her bare legs.

A half-naked girl wearing a very short skirt and almost no top glanced at her. As well as big round earrings in her ears, the girl had a silver earring in her nose, and several rings in each eyebrow.

A boy with wild spiky hair came up behind the girl. And right there, in front of everyone, he kissed her passionately. Right on the lips!

Toby lowered her eyes in embarrassment, and hurried away.

The next shop made her heart leap. There were tables with piles and piles of books with all sorts of colourful covers. She was drawn to the shop like a hungry chicken to fresh grain. She dared herself to touch one of the books with her fingertips. Its cover was smooth and shiny with a picture of children playing with dogs and cats, and there was a lamb and a calf as well. Glory be! She reverently opened the book and sniffed in the new book smell. Her heart raced.

The book was filled with stories about the children and their family on a farm. Toby devoured the stories, one after another. Ira and Mary had a baby sister, Joan. Their father was so amazingly kind to them, and he seemed to have only one wife who was cheerful and kind as well. They were just like the parents in the book Bertha had caught her reading.

Toby's stomach grumbled. Must be almost supper time.

Maybe Jacob and Minerva would be returning to their car. She didn't want them to leave without her. She reluctantly put the book back and made her way out of the mall.

Good, the red Mini was still there, parked in the row closest to the mall's edge. But before she reached it, she spotted the beige van again. She ducked behind a dusty pick-up truck and, with her heart pounding, she crawled into the row of shrubs in the dark shadows beside the mall wall.

She held her breath, wondering if anyone had noticed her. She peeked through the branches. She couldn't see the beige van now. If they did come after her, she would make a run for it. There was no way they were going to catch her and drag her back. She'd rather die. She curled into a ball on the cool dry soil under the prickly branches and waited.

She waited for a long time.

Then she heard voices. Minerva's and Jacob's.

"She's gone, Jay! Toby's gone!"

A car door slammed shut. Then another. The motor started up. The Mini!

Toby caught her breath. The Mini was her only escape. She'd have to chance getting caught.

She hurried out of the shrubs and darted after the small red car, waving her arms frantically. Minerva and Jacob had to see her! They had to stop!

But the Mini continued moving out of the parking lot, following the blue van, down one lane between the parked cars, then another.

Oh no! Minerva and Jacob were leaving without her! They hadn't seen her!

"Stop!" she cried out, racing after them.

The Mini stopped abruptly.

Toby rushed to it and grabbed the door handle.

Jacob stepped out. "Hey, Toby. Come on." He held the door open and waved her inside. "Thought you'd left us."

She scrambled into the backseat and wormed her way under the quilt.

"Quick!" she hissed, panting. "They're after me! I think they saw me."

"Who's they?" Jacob asked her.

"My father. Or maybe some elders from home."

Jacob got in after her and pulled his door shut. Minerva took off after the family van, and out of the parking lot. They followed it into the stream of evening traffic.

Toby peered out the back window.

"What kind of car are they driving?" Jacob asked.

"A beige van. With a big roof rack."

He stared out the back window too. "I don't see any beige van. Do you, Minerva?"

"None that's after us anyway," she said.

Toby couldn't see a beige van following them either. Maybe it hadn't been her father's van after all. She settled into the soft quilt and heaved a big sigh of relief. But her heart was still pounding.

"Who did you say was after you?" Minerva asked her.

"My father. And the elders."

"How would they know you were at the mall? How could they ever follow you here all the way from the Kootenays? Sounds impossible. That's hundreds of kilometers away."

"The elders have lots of spies all over this part of the country," Toby said. "If they want to find out anything at all, they can. They could know exactly where I am."

"I doubt it. There are lots of beige vans around. The one you saw probably belonged to some old farmer. Anyway, I'm glad you didn't get lost." Minerva grinned at her in the rearview mirror, flashing white teeth in a brown face. "We didn't recognize you at first in those clothes."

"Hope you don't mind. I just borrowed them to go into the mall to use the washroom." Toby started to pull off the T-shirt. "I'll put them back into your pack now."

"No, it's okay. Keep them. They're a good disguise. Mom bought me a pile of new clothes. I don't really need those."

"I'd like my cap back though, if you don't mind," Jacob said. "It's my fave. You've got another hat she could borrow, don't you, Min?"

"Sure. My denim sunhat. It's in my pack, Toby. Help yourself."

"Here's some grub. Hope you like chicken." Jacob handed Toby a large sandwich wrapped in foil. It was warm and smelled delicious. "We thought you'd be starving out here."

Toby's eyes stung with tears. She had never met such wonderful, generous kids. She shook her head. As she had suspected for a long time, brown people were no different than white people, no matter what the elders said.

Chapter eight

Jacob reached down for a bottle of water and took a long refreshing drink.

"Maybe Toby would like some water too," Minerva said, so Jacob handed her a bottle as well.

"Blessings," she said, smiling her thanks. She drank the water noisily and brushed the sandwich crumbs off the T-shirt.

After an hour or two driving south, they followed the Max off the main road and down a steep, dusty road into an unexpected hollow in the dry, flat prairie. Set at the bottom of the hollow was an old coal mine village. Small houses and a few shops lined the broad dusty streets.

"Welcome to Carbon," Jacob read the sign. "'Municipal campgrounds, 2 kilometers.' Wonder why Fred decided to camp here for the night. I thought we were heading for Drumheller."

"Mom said they phoned, but couldn't get a spot in the public campground because the Tyrell Dinosaur Museum is there and they don't have a reservation. This one's a lot cheaper anyway."

"That explains it."

They turned into a grassy campground and passed a sign. "Welcome to Carbon Municipal Campgrounds."

"Pretty nice, I'd say," Minerva said as they drove along a bumpy lane to a meandering river.

"Lots of trees at least," Jacob said. He rolled his window right down and took a deep sniff of the cool, fresh-smelling air of twilight.

"I like it here," Toby said. "People won't be able to see us as easily as up on the flat prairie."

"You mean people driving a beige van, don't you?" Minerva said.

Toby just shrugged but didn't say anything.

"Look," Jacob said. "Good big washrooms too. Although after all that swimming, who needs a shower?"

"I would love a shower," Toby said.

"Maybe you could sneak out once it gets dark," Minerva said.

"An excellent field." Jacob got his soccer ball from the floor. "Can't wait to get in a few good kicks."

"How about setting up the tents first?" Minerva said. "I'm helping Mom make supper tonight, so could you set mine up too?"

"Okay, okay."

They parked beside the van and Toby ducked under Minerva's quilt as usual.

"What's for supper?" Jacob asked as he dragged the camping equipment from the trunk to a likely spot not far from the Mini.

"Chili and coleslaw. And a chocolate cake for dessert," his mom said from the picnic table where she was setting up the gas stove and supplies.

"Yum!"

Jacob had both tents up in a few minutes while Barney and Sam argued as usual, about who should do what. Minerva had gone to the washroom and Mom was stirring the chili in a big pot on the camp stove. Now was his chance. He could tell her about their stowaway. He opened his mouth, but Toby's tear-smeared face popped into his head. "Please don't tell anyone," she had begged. He hesitated. Then he said, "I'm just going over to that playing field to kick the ball around."

"Don't be long," his mom said. "Supper should be ready in twenty minutes."

Jacob jogged around the grassy area, dribbling his ball back and forth, back and forth across the field. Soon sweat was trickling down his forehead and his neck. It was a good sweat from exercise. But there was still that hollow in his stomach. He hated being dishonest with his mom.

Sam called him. "Jay! Your mom said to tell you that supper's ready now."

Supper of chili and big crusty buns was extra delicious.

"Enough for seconds?" Barney asked.

"Seconds for anyone who wants to clean the pot," Jacob's mom told him.

"Hand that pot over."

"Remember when you hated spicy food?" Jacob said.

"That was ages ago when I didn't know any better," Barney said. "This chili is fantastic."

"Why, thank you, Barney," Jacob's mom said, smiling at him. "This cook always enjoys a compliment."

Jacob grinned at Barney too. It wasn't the first time he'd noticed that the Finkles had become used to his mom's spicy Jamaican cooking.

There was one crusty roll left which Minerva buttered and added a thick wedge of cheese and a spoonful of chili. Jacob knew who that would be for. For a second he felt guilty about enjoying supper so much while Toby was huddled in the backseat of the Mini without a thing to eat. He nudged his ball from under the table and it rolled out. As he bent to pick it up and go continue kicking it around, Fred said, "How about a dip in the river before it gets too dark?"

"Count me out," Jacob groaned. "I'm still waterlogged from the pool at the mall."

"Me too," Sam said.

"Think I'll take the kayak in for a spin," Fred said.

"Hey, you guys heard about the horse that named both his sons Ed?" Barney geared himself up for another practice session of horse jokes and riddles. "Because you all know that two 'Eds' are better than one. Get it? Two 'Eds'? Two 'Eds'?"

Jacob groaned. Here we go again, he thought. "Hey, Fred," he said. "Need a hand getting the boat off the car?"

Anything to avoid another session of Barney's tired humour.

🚗 🚗 🚗

That night Toby was snuggled on the backseat of the Mini under Minerva's quilt. Her stomach ached with hunger. The bun and cheese Minerva had brought her earlier had just whetted her appetite.

From her nest, she could see out the rear window. She stared up through the leafy branches to the black sky and twinkling stars.

She didn't like looking at the stars because, what if they started falling, as the prophet had said they would at the end of the world? That moment could come any time at all now, he had predicted. Maybe right in the very next second. She squeezed her eyes shut and held her breath. Nothing happened except a breeze blew through the open window and some crickets chirped.

She tossed and wiggled around trying to find a more comfortable spot on the crowded backseat. Her stomach was so empty it actually gurgled.

One thing about living in the commune with all her brothers and sisters and step-mothers, there was always enough food. It wasn't fancy, but it was tasty and plentiful. They had three big meals a day which she helped prepare. She and Ellie, one of her half-sisters, had been on potato duty last month and they had to peel mountains of potatoes every night. She remembered how she and Ellie had giggled, and how Big Bad Bertha had scolded them.

"Kitchen work is serious work. The devil finds work for idle hands. Get busy now, girls. No more fooling."

Toby wasn't used to this empty hollow feeling of hunger. But she wasn't sorry for an instant that she had run away from the commune. The prospect of the elders' plans for her was too terrible to think about for even a minute.

She shook her head to push away the unwelcome thoughts. "Think about food instead," she told herself. "Spicy cabbage rolls, crispy fried chicken, and vegetables fresh from their gardens, crunchy cucumbers and sweet tomatoes. Fresh baked bread still warm from the oven with melted butter and strawberry jam. Yum!"

Her stomach gurgled again. There must be some food around here somewhere.

She stared out all the car windows. No one was in sight. It looked as though everyone in the camp had gone to sleep in their tents or RVs. No lights were on anywhere except the washroom. She was even too hungry now to contemplate a shower.

She climbed into the front seat. Any food there? Just an old dried-up apple core in the garbage bag. Did she dare leave the car? A pain stabbed her side. Hunger. She held onto her side and cautiously pushed the door open. She eased herself outside. It was cooler out here. The night breeze found her back and bare legs immediately. She crossed her arms tightly to trap the warmth under her T-shirt and sidled between the cars and tents.

Where could she find some food? She could see the family's picnic table in the moonlight. An oblong box on it looked like a camp stove. Beside it was a small cooler. Must be something to eat in there. She sneaked across the damp grass, drawn to the cooler like a fly to a sticky jam pot.

She lifted the lid but couldn't see much in the darkness. She felt around the various lumps. Eggs, a jug of milk maybe. Then she felt something with a round top. She lifted out a carton. What was in it? She pried off the lid, dipped in her finger and tasted. Sweet and tangy. Maybe she'd have just a little bit. She raised the carton to her lips and slurped up the contents. Oh, yum! So smooth and delicious. She slurped some more and soon it was all gone. She ran her finger around the sides to get the last bit. Should she put the empty carton back into the cooler?

Before she decided, the sound of footsteps swished along the lane between the campsites. She crept back to the Mini and slipped inside, still clutching the container and ducked under Minerva's quilt before anyone saw her.

She took a deep breath. That delicious food had filled the emptiness in her stomach. "Praise be to God," she prayed as she snuggled back into her warm nest and tumbled into a deep sleep.

Chapter nine

The next morning, Jacob's mother said, "Funny. I was sure there was a full carton of yogurt in the cooler to have with our cereal. It seems to have disappeared."

"Don't worry, Rosa, my dear," Fred said. "We'll get more supplies when we're in Drumheller later today."

Jacob caught Minerva's eye. She nodded. They knew where the yogurt must have gone.

When they left the campground, the Mini following the Max as usual, the road was so dusty they had to roll up the windows.

"Okay back there?" Minerva asked Toby.

"I'm fine, thanks."

It was a relief to get to the paved streets of Drumheller finally.

"They built this town in a hollow like they did for Carbon," Jacob said, rolling down his window and taking in a deep breath of fresh air.

"One way of getting away from that nasty prairie wind," Minerva said.

"Looks a lot bigger than Carbon," Jacob said, as they parked near the Max in the parking lot beside a tourist office.

"Sorry, but it's going be hot for you in the car," Minerva said to Toby. "I'll leave the windows open so you can get some air. And here's an extra bottle of water."

"Thanks," Toby said. She'd already ducked under the quilt.

"Minerva," Fred said as she and Jacob joined the rest of the family. "You forgot to shut your windows. You can't leave the car unlocked around here. Someone may steal it."

"Silly me," Minerva said, and went back to the car to roll up the windows.

Jacob followed the rest of the family out of the parking lot. It was a hot day and with the windows tightly closed, the girl would end up roasting. He looked around for something to distract the family so the girl could open the windows without them noticing.

A huge model of a dinosaur stood on the other side of the tourist office.

"Wow! Will you look at that sucker!" Jacob said. "Must be fifty meters high, at least."

Sam came around the corner and his eyes popped. "Wow-ie!" he breathed.

"Now that's what I call a gi-normous beast," Barney said.

They all stared up at a huge model of a Tyrannosaurus Rex. Jacob had never seen any model so big and so realistic. It towered ferociously over the tourist office building.

"A perfect spot for a family photograph," Fred said, rummaging around for his camera and tripod. "Come, everyone. Let's get ourselves organized."

So they all had to gather around the base of the huge model.

Jacob leaned against T-Rex's big toe. The sun blazed down right on his head. It was uncomfortable out here, but he couldn't imagine how hot Toby must be, stuck in the backseat of the Mini. On the other hand, it was her choice, he reminded himself.

Fred took forever setting up his equipment. He fiddled with his camera and the tripod, pushing it up and down.

Jacob wished he'd brought along his hat. Maybe he'd have time to zip back to the Mini to get it.

Then Fred said, "Okay. It's all set. Come on now. Can't you at least look as if you're enjoying all this?"

Jacob groaned and tried to find a bit of shade, but there was none except a small triangle where Sam was crouched, between two of the dinosaur's long toes.

"I can't see you, Sam," Fred called. "You'll have to move forward."

Sam slouched in front of Jacob and stepped on Barney's foot.

"Hey, watch out, Squirt!" Barney shoved his brother.

Sam squawked and fell to his knees.

"Now, now, Sam. Be sensible," his father said. "We'll never get this photograph taken."

"Come and stand near me." Minerva put her arm around Sam's shoulders and pulled him close. He looked up at her and leaned into her side. Minerva always had a way with Sam.

A line of tourists formed behind Fred and gawked at them.

Jacob wished they'd just disappear. Why do people always have to stare at us like that? It made him feel on display, like a monkey in a cage. Had they never seen a multicoloured family get their photo taken before? He'd stick out his tongue at them, but that would probably make them stare even harder.

"Okay, this is it. Just stay right there," Fred called out, pressing the shutter and sprinting to them. He placed himself beside Jacob's mom. "Don't move a bloomin' muscle now except your smile muscles."

The camera blinked a few times.

"Big smiles," Jacob's mom said. "As if you're all really enjoying our wonderful family holiday."

Jacob pushed his lips up into a phony smile that was more of a grimace. A rivulet of sweat trickled down his cheek but he didn't dare move to brush it away. He just wanted to get this torture over and done with.

Finally the camera flashed.

"Right-o!" Fred said. "I'm sure that photograph will be excellent."

"Can we go to the dinosaur museum now, Dad?" Sam whined.

🚗 🚗 🚗

In the parking lot, Toby peeked out through the Mini's back window. Jacob and Minerva and their family had gathered at the base of the enormous green dinosaur. They were all dressed in short-sleeved shirts and shorts except the mother who was wearing a flowered skirt and a pink blouse. Jacob was restless, obviously uncomfortable. He stood beside the boy with spiky red hair and glasses, almost his height. That would be Barney. Jacob frowned as his brown face glistened with sweat and he pulled back his long ringlets. She had never known anyone before who looked like him. Or Minerva. Or their mother. Staring at Jacob made Toby's heart beat faster. He was so handsome.

Minerva pulled the younger boy closer, and pointed to the camera. That must be Sam. He seemed to like Minerva very much. They all turned towards the father behind his camera, their faces frozen into smiles.

Toby grinned as the father's long legs flew while he loped clumsily to join the rest of the family. He put his arm around Minerva's mother, drew her close and she smiled up at him and stroked his beard. They turned to the camera, their faces in matching smiles. They all waited a moment, rigid. There was a flash, then they all relaxed and started talking and laughing.

Toby's eyes stung. How she longed to be part of a family like that. Brothers and a sister, a jolly father, and just one mother. And all so loving and obviously enjoying each other. Instead of what she had. As long as she could remember, she had never been on a family holiday. She had so many half-sisters and half-brothers, forty-eight, including her and all her father's sister-wives' children. How could they even fit into one photograph? Practically the only time she ever saw her father was on Sundays at church services or when she had to go to him for a reprimand or a beating, like that night when Big B.B. had caught her reading that book. Even her own mother didn't always acknowledge her. She was just another mouth to feed, and another back to put clothes onto, and another pair of hands to work in the kitchen or the fields, and another . . . No, she told herself. She refused to think about *that*.

🚗 🚗 🚗

After the scorching heat of the day, the Royal Tyrell Dinosaur Museum felt like a cool haven to Jacob. It was like stepping into a dim ancient rainforest world of giant ferns and tall trees where the mighty dinosaurs once ruled. Jacob took in a deep breath of the moist air. It smelled sweet and pungent.

He laughed at Sam. Sam was so excited he couldn't move. He stood stunned at the entrance, gazing at the displays, his eyes huge. Then he drifted inside slowly as if in a dream. "Oh, man!" he breathed. "I heard this museum was good, but never expected it to be this fantastic."

"Wake up, Sammy," Jacob said, patting his back. "You're really here. This is the real thing."

Sam turned round and round. He didn't know where to start. He wanted to examine every single thing all at once. He dashed to the first huge skeleton, then to the next, and the next, reading out the information in a loud excited voice.

Fred shared his enthusiasm.

In the end, even Jacob had to admit it was a cool display.

"I agree," Minerva said to him. "Just look at the size of that triceratops. I never realized they were that huge, but it says here that the model is life-sized."

Jacob followed her and his mom around the dim area, staring at the enormous animals and lush vegetation. Barney trailed after them. When they eventually wandered to the end of the meandering path between the displays, they could see that Fred and Sam weren't even half-way through the museum yet.

"Think I've had enough," Minerva said. "I'm going back to the car."

"Don't you want to check out the gift shop?" their mom said.

Minerva shrugged and followed her into the gift shop. But she was frowning. Jacob knew what she was thinking about. Their stowaway. He followed them and so did Barney.

"Wow!" Barney gazed around the gift shop. "I've never seen so much dinosaur stuff in my whole entire life."

Jacob stared at the rows and shelves crammed with dinosaur figures, dinosaur posters, books, puzzles and games and fancy dinosaur T-shirts, and hats, kites and key-chains, balls, pens and erasers. Every possible dinosaur object imaginable was there.

Barney fell upon the books. "You won't believe what they've got here!" he called out to Jacob.

"What?"

"*Giant Dinosaur Joke Book*! What could be better? You're probably right about horses not being all that funny. But what about dinosaurs? Now, jokes about dinosaurs must have plenty of appeal."

Jacob just shook his head.

Barney enthusiastically flipped through the thick book. "Okay, how about this one? Did you hear about the Albertosaurus who lost 30 pounds on an all-popcorn diet? Problem was, he had to spend $6000 going to movies."

Jacob's mom laughed. "That's a pretty good joke, Barney. I like that."

"Oh, please," Jacob groaned. "Don't encourage him."

"What about this one? How did Iguanodons catch flies?"

"I don't know," Jacob's mom said. "How?"

"With baseball gloves! Ooo! I love it! I love it!" Barney hopped around in excited circles. "I could get a real dynamite routine going with these dinosaur riddles. I'd get myself a cool dinosaur mask, and—"

"So you're asking me to buy the book for you?" Jacob's mom said.

"Would you? I'll give you the money when we get back to the van. I left my wallet there."

"I'm going to the car," Minerva said.

"I'd like to drive the Mini for awhile," their mother said, rooting around in her purse for some money for Barney. "Give you a break, Min. Would you mind?"

"Mind? Oh no. Not a bit," Minerva said.

But a look of panic flashed across her face.

Jacob knew what she was thinking. What if Mom finds out about Toby?

Chapter ten

"Barney, would you go and tell your father that we'll be waiting for him out in the parking lot?" Jacob's mom asked.

Minerva said, "Before we go, let's get some cold bottled water, Mom. Sure am thirsty."

"Good idea. I'll buy a big jug. Then everyone can fill their water bottles. We must remember to keep hydrated with all this heat."

While their mom was getting the water jug from the cooler, Minerva gave Jacob her car key. "Want to go warn you-know-who?"

"Still think we should tell Mom."

"We can't," Minerva said. "Toby must have her reasons to stay hidden and we should respect that. Don't you see?"

"Okay, okay," he sighed. "I'll go along with it, but I'm not happy. We still don't even really know why she ran away."

"All those scratches and bruises make me think she was beaten up a lot, which probably has something to do with it. She'll tell us when she's ready. I'm sure she will."

Jacob nodded and sprinted out to where they'd parked the car in the shade of a spindly tree. He peered into the back window. Toby was lying on the backseat, fast asleep. Her face was flushed with heat although she had opened both front windows for air. When he unlocked the door, she woke with a start and stared at him.

"My mom's going to be driving the Mini for awhile," he told her in a low voice.

"Oh no!"

"If you don't want her to see you, you'll have to stay under the quilt."

Toby quickly disappeared under the quilt. And just in time, because his mom and Minerva arrived, carrying the jug of cold water.

"Haven't driven my little Mini for ages." Their mom patted the roof as if it was a friendly family pet. "I must say I'll surely miss it this winter."

"I promise I'll take very good care of it," Minerva said, her eyes wandering to the backseat for any sign of Toby. "Want to fill your water bottle from this jug, Jay?"

"Sure."

The Finkles soon joined them. Sam was clutching two new dinosaur figures from the gift shop.

"We should check the map to see where to head next," Fred said, reaching into the van for his road map.

"I'm going to drive the Mini for awhile," Jacob's mom said.

"Right-o. Should we continue along the minor roads? They're usually a lot more interesting."

"Fine with me."

"Did you see that fabulous Albertosaurus?" Sam said. "They found those actual bones right near here in the Bad Lands just south of Drumheller. Can you believe it? Dad said that when I'm older, I can come out to a dig. And maybe I'll find some dinosaur bones too. The guide in there said that kids often do." His face was flushed with excitement and he just couldn't stop talking.

Jacob leaned on the Mini. He couldn't face hearing any more about dinosaurs at the moment, so he'd opt to stay in the little car with his mom driving. He got in, pulled his door shut and leaned back, buckling up his seatbelt while his mom got in and started the car. He held his breath. Would she find out about Toby? If she did, he knew he'd be in big trouble for deceiving her.

Once they were on their way, he listened hard and heard only the rumble of the motor and the swish of the breeze blowing in the windows. So far, so good.

After a quick trip to a supermarket, they were back on the

road, driving away from Drumheller. But the Max stirred up the dust on the road.

"All this dust," Jacob's mom said. "Roll up the windows."

While she was talking, Jacob heard Toby sneeze! Then she sneezed again.

Oh no! His mom would hear! He grabbed a wad of tissue from the box and stuffed it in front of his nose, pretending to have a sneezing fit.

"Jacob!" His mom was alarmed. "What's the matter, my sweet? All that sneezing. I hope you're not catching a cold."

"It's nothing." He held the tissue to his nose. "Just this dusty road."

"I'll make you some of my special Jamaican cold remedy tonight," she said. "That will fix you up in two-twos. You'll see."

He grimaced at the thought of her fiery concoction of pepper sauce, ginger, onion and squeezed garlic juice.

"I'm feeling better already," he assured her. "How about some good Jamaican music?"

"Oh, please," she said. "I'd love it!"

Jacob rummaged through their CDs and found Burning Spear. He put it in the player and cranked up the volume. Now if Toby had another sneezing fit, his mom wouldn't hear her.

After they had gone on for quite awhile, bouncing and singing along with the lively reggae music, up and down the rolling hills covered with fields of long grass and scrub and the occasional farm, Fred pulled the van over to the side of the road in front of a painted billboard. Jacob's mom tucked the Mini in behind.

Fred jumped out of the van and called to them enthusiastically, "What do you think of that, Rosa? A whole museum of bloomin' prairie dogs dressed up as all sorts of people like Red Riding Hood, and all the presidents of the United States from George Washington as well as all the prime ministers of Canada from Sir John A! Blimey! That must be some exhibit!"

"Fine, Fred. Lead on," Jacob's mom said. "We'll follow."

When they were on the road again, Jacob said, "Mom, do we really have to go to that museum?"

"The whole thing does sound ghastly, doesn't it? Maybe there will be a good field nearby where you can kick around your soccer ball instead."

They turned off the road into the village and stopped again. This time, near a sign that announced, "Prairie Dog Museum, 200 meters. You are almost there." Beside the sign was a colourful painting of prairie dogs dressed up as cowboys with cowboy hats and boots and everything.

Fred strode back to the Mini with long excited steps. "Just imagine dressing prairie dogs like cowboys rounding up cattle. Now that must be really something!"

"We're right behind you, my sweet," Jacob's mom said.

When they drove into the museum parking lot, there was a sign on the entrance. "Closed Mondays."

"Festeration!" Fred ranted, waving his fist. "How can they expect to make any bloomin' money with an enterprise that's closed for the day? Right in the middle of the tourist season. Whatever's happened to good old free enterprise?"

"How about some ice cream, instead?" Jacob's mom said. "I bet we could get some in that village grocery store across the street."

And she was right. As far as Jacob was concerned, a chocolate ripple ice cream cone beat a mind-numbing museum any day. Especially one populated by dressed-up dead prairie dogs.

As he licked the chocolatey sweetness of the ice cream, he was aware of their silent passenger in the backseat. She sure would like some of this cool delicious treat. He just couldn't think of a way to get it to her without his mom finding out about her. Well, it was Toby's idea to keep her presence a secret. As far as he was concerned, they should have told their mom about her right from the beginning.

"What's the matter, Jay?" his mom asked. "I thought chocolate ripple was your favourite."

"Oh, right." Melted ice cream was trickling down his fingers. He quickly licked it up. He could pass Toby a water bottle, at least. But he'd have to think of something to distract his mom. "Oh, look, a hawk!" he said, pointing out at the side of the road.

When she stared out at the big bird perched on a power pole, he slipped a bottle of water under the quilt on the backseat.

"A huge beauty," his mom said. "Doing a great job catching the mice that eat farmers' crops."

"Right," Jacob said, turning up the reggae music.

They carried on, travelling east along a paved but quiet road that crossed the rolling Alberta prairie, following a line of power cables strung between wooden poles that marched off to the distant horizon.

"We're getting low on gas so how about calling Fred on the walkie-talkie to stop at the next gas station," Jacob's mom said.

Jacob called and they stopped at a gas station on the outskirts of a village where they all got out to stretch.

"Hey, Jay," Barney said. "Why don't dinosaurs get up and leave the museum?"

"Don't know, Barney. Why?"

"They just don't have the guts. Get it? They don't have the guts?"

"Yeah, I get it. I get it."

"How's it going?" Minerva asked him in a low voice.

He knew she was asking about their stowaway. "Okay, so far," he said.

"What's okay?" Barney asked, poking his pointy nose into their business.

They were beside a notice board in front of the gas station. "Look," Jacob said to distract him. "Says here that they have a B&B in the next town, Dora's B&B, and they allow camping in their yard."

"Reasonable rates," Fred read over Jacob's shoulder. "Sounds absolutely perfect to me."

They soon saw a small sign at the side of the road. "Dora's

B&B and camping," so they turned off, bounced over some railway tracks, and found a village of maybe ten houses, one small general store, and a tall grain elevator rising from the middle of a farmer's field.

It didn't take long to figure out where Dora's B&B was. They just followed the signs to the farm next to the grain elevator.

They drove into a yard cluttered with small buildings and farm equipment surrounding a modern farm house. An older woman wearing an apron over her dress hurried out of the house, the screen door slamming behind her.

"Welcome!" she greeted them, smiling.

"I'm just curious," Fred said. "How did that grain elevator get there? I thought they were always next to the train tracks."

"It's a long story," the woman said. "Turns out they were going to demolish it. Didn't need it any more, they said, now they have a new and improved one a few miles down the road."

"Right," Fred said. "I think we saw it."

"So my husband, who can't stand waste, moved it out back. Said it would be a tourist attraction."

"Is that so! Sure would have liked to have seen it."

"They just put it up on rollers, and pulled it along with the tractor, smooth as cream. A few boards came loose, but they soon fixed them up."

"Must have been quite a sight! We'd like to camp tonight. Do you have room?"

"Sure thing," the woman said. "No one else is camping at the moment so you'll have the place to yourselves. Just pull your cars to the other side of the grain elevator and come back up to the house to sign up."

The grass was spiky on the shady side of the grain elevator, but it was cooler and out of the wind. There were several new picnic tables and fire pits, and as the woman had said, they had the place to themselves.

"The guys' turn to cook supper tonight," Jacob's mom informed everyone. "We've got the fixings for hamburgers."

"Hey, Jay," Barney said. "That's our specialty."

"Right. You'll have to pitch the tents on your own, Minerva."

"No problem."

One thing Jacob was glad about: his mom had forgotten about making her nasty-tasting concoction for his supposed cold. He didn't mind onions when they were fried up with peppers. He liked their tangy smell and how they popped around in the frying pan. The hamburger patties were pre-formed so it was easy just to fry them as well, while Barney sliced the buns and tomatoes.

"Should I mix some of my special sauce?" he asked, reaching for the ketchup, relish and mayonnaise.

"Sure thing," Jacob said, flipping over the burgers.

"So do you know why so few dinosaurs flew?" Barney asked.

Here we go again, Jacob groaned. "No, why?"

"Because they couldn't fit into the cockpit."

"Ah, good one," Jacob said, humouring him.

"How about this one? Why did the Brachiosaurus have such a long neck?"

"Don't know. Maybe to eat leaves from tall trees like giraffes do?"

"No. He had to have a long neck because his head was so far from his body. Get it? Far from his body?"

"Oh, right. Good one too. Say, is that sauce ready? These burgers are."

"Yup," Barney said. "Supper's ready," he announced to everyone else.

It was getting dark, so Fred lit a lantern for the middle of the picnic table. Everyone piled their plates with thick burgers, baby carrots and celery and taco chips.

"These hamburgers are bloomin' perfect." Fred wiped sauce off his beard with his handkerchief. "Are there seconds?"

"Seconds coming right up." Jacob flipped a couple more patties into the pan. "Anyone else want one."

"I'll have another," Minerva said.

"You're not even finished your first one," their mother said.

"I soon will be," Minerva said.

But Jacob knew who that second burger was really for. Minerva would find some way to sneak it out to the Mini for Toby.

"Reminds me of another dinosaur riddle," Barney said.

Everyone groaned.

"Okay. Here it is. Was anyone safe from man-eating dinosaurs?"

"Sure," Sam said. "Everyone was, because no people were around when the dinosaurs were here. Everyone knows that."

"The correct answer is," Barney said, frowning at his brother, "all women and children were safe. Get it? Man-eating dinosaurs would eat just men, not women and children. So of course, they'd all be safe."

"But I told you, no people were around when dinosaurs were here," Sam insisted. "Don't you know anything at all about dinosaurs?"

"Anyone have room for dessert? Apple pie and yogurt?" Jacob's mom interrupted before Sam and Barney started throttling each other.

After supper, Fred said, "Since we didn't prepare this feast, Sam, my boy, we're on washing-up duty."

Jacob slipped Minerva the extra burger which she wrapped in a napkin and stashed under the front of her hoodie. As she turned to escape to the Mini, Barney said, "Hey, Min. You know why a Brachiosaurus's head was so far from its body?"

She turned back, holding her arm close to her side so the burger wouldn't fall out. "I don't know. Why?"

"Because its neck is so long. No, no, that's not right. Goes like this: Do you know why a Brachiosaurus had such a long neck?"

She shook her head.

"Because its head was so far from its body. Want to hear another one?"

Minerva looked at Jacob, pleading with her eyes.

"Hey, Barn," he said. "You checked out the grain elevator yet?"

"No, not yet."

"Grab your towel and let's go. The woman said there were showers. And after that hot day, us guys can sure all use one, right?"

Minerva sent Jacob a grateful smile.

The grain elevator was huge. The bottom floor had been divided into two washrooms, one for men and one for women.

"Sure would like to climb to the top," Barney said. "Bet you'd have a great view of the whole prairies."

"No stairs going up. Too bad. I'm trying out the showers. You?"

"Okay. I guess. Say, did you hear the one about the . . ."

"Give it a rest, will you? No more jokes or riddles for tonight, okay?"

Chapter eleven

Toby closed her eyes as she bit into the hamburger. "Mmm. This has to be the most blissful food I've ever had in my whole entire life. Bless you. Bless you," she said to Minerva. The juicy sauce ran down her chin so she had to use Minerva's T-shirt to wipe it up. Good thing it was black and wouldn't show the stains too much.

She was crouched down beside the backseat, while Minerva sat in the front, pretending to read a magazine with her flashlight in case anyone looked their way.

"You can thank my brother. He and Barney made supper tonight." Her feeble light glinted off her gold earrings.

"Boys cooking a meal? Oh my! Now that would never happen at home. Only girls and women prepare meals. Men don't ever cook, not even a snack. Surely am thirsty and I would be grateful for something to drink."

"Here's a bottle with a bit of water. I could get you more. Or you could get some yourself at the washroom. There's a shower there too, if you want a shower later."

"I would love a shower. I got so hot and sticky today. Do you think it will be safe?"

"Sure. The washroom's always open so you could go when everyone's asleep. There's an extra towel in my pack, and some shampoo. Help yourself." Minerva brushed out her long curly hair and pulled it back with a clip. "Hope you're okay sleeping back there."

"It's fine," Toby said. "Cozy."

"Okay. Good night then."

"Good night. And thank you."

Minerva left to get settled in her tent for the night.

Toby was still hungry after the burger, but she was even thirstier. She drained the water bottle Minerva had given her. After a while, there was no movement around the camp and it looked as though everyone had gone to bed. Could she chance going for a shower now?

She rummaged around Minerva's pack and came up with a towel and a small bottle of shampoo. She buckled on her sandals, quietly opened the car door and slipped out. She stopped to listen. All was silent except for the hum of crickets. She hurried across the dark path of spiky grass to the grain elevator. As Minerva had said, there were showers and they were lovely. Toby had a long drink and let the warm water spray over her head and down her back to the welts where her father had whipped her. The blessed water soothed her bruises and scratches and after awhile, she felt as blissfully clean as clean could be.

After she had dried off, she didn't want to put on the sweaty T-shirt and shorts she had borrowed from Minerva, but she had no choice. That's all she had. She could rinse out her underwear though, so she did it in the sink.

She wrapped the towel around her hair and pushed the door open to leave, forgetting to check for anyone. Oh no! A man with a flashlight was coming up the path towards the grain elevator. She caught her breath and froze. What could she do? He had seen her!

"Good evening, young lady," the man said gruffly. He had a beard and was wearing a hat. "I thought we were the only family camping here tonight."

"Ah . . ." Toby couldn't think of anything to say. She turned and slipped back into the washroom. She rushed into a toilet cubicle and locked it. Her heart raced. That was Fred, who was married to Minerva's mother. And he'd seen her! What could she do now?

She stayed in the cubicle for a long while, trying to decide. Maybe she should crawl out the back window and make a run for it into the fields.

On the other hand, how would he know who she was or where she had been hiding?

All was quiet. She crept to the door and opened it a slit. No one was there now so she slipped out and hurried back to the Mini. She dove into the backseat and buried herself under the quilt.

It took a long time for her heart to settle down and her breathing to return to normal. She kept expecting to see Fred's bearded face staring at her through one of the car windows.

🚗 🚗 🚗

The next morning the family had pancakes with special Saskatoon berry syrup they had bought from Dora, the B&B woman.

"Bloomin' delicious syrup," Fred declared. "Seems to be a cross between blueberry and blackberry, I reckon. We should get another couple of bottles. By the way, a strange thing happened last night. I was on my way to the washroom when I saw a girl coming out of the ladies'. I thought we were the only ones camping here. She was small, around ten or eleven, I'd say. Much too young to be on her own."

"Maybe she's one of Dora's grandchildren," Minerva said.

Jacob knew right away who it really was.

"This girl looked mighty scared when she saw me," Fred said. "She ran back and hid in the washroom."

"Maybe she's just shy," Minerva said. "Maybe kids around here don't have much chance to meet many people."

"What did she look like?" their mom asked.

"Hard to tell in the dark. And she had a towel on her head so I couldn't see her hair. Wonder if we should tell Dora about her."

"Maybe she's staying at the B&B and the showers there were all busy," Jacob said.

A worried frown puckered Minerva's forehead.

"Who's for another pancake?" she asked, brandishing the pancake flipper.

Of course Fred wanted more. And so did Barney and Sam. You could always distract the Finkles with the promise of food.

Chapter twelve

"Looks as if Saskatoon will be our next stop," Fred said, shaking out the tourist map of Saskatchewan, and laying it out flat on the picnic table. "Listen to this. 'The Western Development Museum. A fascinating look at Saskatchewan's past. 1910 boom town.'" He closed the guide book. "Now that sounds even more interesting than a bunch of stuffed prairie dogs, don't you all think? And we're not that far away from it."

Jacob's mom said, "Might be a good break from driving all the time."

"I think I even heard that the museum is free," Fred said.

Well, that decided it.

When they finally arrived in Saskatoon, they found it was a small city with the main highway going through the middle of it.

Minerva was back driving the Mini, following the Max as usual. They drove across town, over a bridge that spanned the South Saskatchewan River, and finally came to the museum.

"Not many cars here," Jacob said. "Guess the Western Development Museum isn't the most popular spot in town."

"It's early yet," Minerva said, as she parked at the edge of a big dusty parking lot. "Sorry, Toby. Not much shade around here."

"I will be fine," Toby said, checking out the other cars in the parking lot. "At least there aren't any beige vans from BC here."

"You're not still worried that your father has managed to track you all across the prairies, are you?" Minerva asked.

Toby shrugged. "I wouldn't be surprised. There are Brethren everywhere. Could I read one of your magazines while you're gone?"

"Sure. Help yourself. I'll leave the windows open so you can at least get some fresh air."

As they were walking to the museum, Fred said, "Minerva, you forgot to roll up your windows again. You won't hang onto that car long if you don't lock it up properly, you know."

"Oh, that's right," she said, about to return to the Mini.

"I'll do it," Jacob said. "Forgot my wallet."

"Sorry," he said to Toby, as he rolled the windows back up. "I know it's going to be hot in here, but Fred said we had to shut the windows. Once we're inside, you can lower them again, okay?"

The girl's cheeks were already flushed red from the heat.

🚗 🚗 🚗

"What?" Fred exclaimed loudly. "Ten dollars each! I was told this museum was free."

"Perhaps you have this museum confused with our provincial museum in Regina, sir. That one is free," the attendant said. She was a prissy older woman, with grey hair piled up in a tight bun, and she was dressed in an old-fashioned dress with long skirts and lots of fancy white lace around the top.

Jacob nudged Minerva. Frugal Fred. At least this time no one was waiting in line behind them.

"Driving all the way to Regina would be too far for us today," Fred said. "Surely, you must at least have a family rate, madam?"

"We do, but it's for one family." The woman looked pointedly at the pale Barney and Sam, and then at the darker Jacob, Minerva and their mom.

Jacob's face flushed and he yanked one of his dreadlocks.

He knew she was wondering how they could all belong to the same family with all their different shades. Everyone always did.

Fred became exasperated. "Not again. Look, madam. This is my family." He turned to Jacob's mom. "Next time remind me to bring along our bloomin' marriage certificate."

"Now, Fred," she said, patting his hand.

The woman attendant sighed. "Fine then," she said through tight lips. "One family pass for you."

Jacob followed his mom as they all filed past the attendant's disapproving gaze into a large darkened room.

"Not exactly one of your most friendly of hosts," Jacob's mom commented to him.

Jacob could see that his mom was embarrassed. He hated it when that happened. "Look," he said. "They've got a whole village built in here."

"A village as it would have looked in 1910, about a hundred years ago," his mom read.

There weren't many people in the museum, which was built inside a huge warehouse. A wooden boardwalk was lined with standing flickering gas lamps and small shops, and old-fashioned automobiles were parked along a road.

Barney skipped on ahead. "Wow, look! Look at all these bicycles, Dad! And a, a . . . what do you call those bikes with that big front wheel and tiny back one?"

"Penny Farthings," Fred read out from the information board in an embarrassingly loud voice that echoed up to the high darkened ceiling. "Invented in 1870, and called the 'Ordinary' bicycle for many years until this other one was invented in 1887 by John Kemp Starley." He patted the worn leather seat of a bicycle that looked more modern, with its two wheels the same size and a chain going from the pedals to the back wheel.

"Now this one is much easier and safer to ride because your feet are closer to the ground, so if you fall off, you don't have so blasted far to fall," he lectured. "That's why they were called 'Safety' bicycles. Just getting up onto this Penny Farthing to ride it is a challenge."

"How did they do that, Dad?" Barney asked.

"I believe you had to get onto it from the rear by putting one foot on this bolt like this." Fred reached up to grip the high seat. "Then you'd have to hoist yourself up onto the seat like this and . . ." From his perch on the high seat, Fred looked startled as the bicycle inched forward off its stand.

Then suddenly, the bicycle swooshed away. "Blood and guts!" Fred cried out in a panic as the tall bicycle shot forward and zigzagged across the street.

"Dad!" yelled Barney.

"Dad!" yelled Sam. "Da-ad!"

"Excuse me, sir!" A pudgy guard rushed after him. "Sir! The exhibits aren't to be ridden, sir! Sir! Sir!"

"Fred! Come back, dearest!" Jacob's mom shouted. "Come back!"

"Dad! Dad!" Sam cried, running after him.

Jacob didn't know what to do. He watched them all rushing after the wobbly bicycle. It swerved from one side of the street to the other, and back again while Fred struggled frantically with the handle bars.

"Festeration!" he shouted. "Can't get this blasted . . ."

With a loud crash, the bicycle bashed into a pile of wooden barrels. Fred landed, sprawled out on the street, barrels thumping and rolling around him.

"Oh, no!" Minerva groaned.

Jacob fought an urge to laugh.

The guard caught up to Fred who was lying on the ground, elbows and knees sticking out. "Sir! Are you all right, sir?"

"Dad! Dad!" Barney and Sam rushed to him.

Jacob's mom hurried to Fred too. "Oh, you poor, poor man!" she murmured, bending over him. "Are you hurt, my dearest?"

Fred shook his head as he untangled his long hairy legs from the huge wheel. She helped him up and brushed the dust off his shirt, tut-tutting her concern.

"As I said," the guard wheezed, "these exhibits are strictly for display purposes, sir. The bicycles are certainly not meant to be ridden."

"Very sorry," Fred apologized. "I was just demonstrating to my family here, how these Penny Farthings work. Amazing machines! I'm just curious, sir, but do you have any printed information about this one?"

He was obviously unhurt so Jacob followed Minerva as she jogged away along the boardwalk, her sandals slapping the boards and echoing hollowly in the darkness.

Jacob was glad to escape from the embarrassing Fred Finkle, and Co. He peered into Ming's Laundry, one of the musty old shops that lined the street. "Cool," he said to Minerva. "Imagine what life would have been like a hundred years ago. Whenever you wanted a clean pair of underwear, you'd have to drag your laundry to a shop like this."

Minerva shrugged impatiently. She was on edge and went through the historical displays quickly. Jacob tagged after her. They came to a tiny movie theatre where they sat on a wooden bench and watched a shadowy Charlie Chaplin movie where Charlie moved jerkily across the screen, trying to get away from the bad guys, accompanied by peppy organ music. After a while, their mother joined them, sighing and putting up her feet.

Minerva swung her legs restlessly. She got up and paced the aisle.

"What's the matter, girl?" her mom asked her. "Why don't you just relax? Is something bothering you?"

"Don't you think we should be heading back to the cars now?"

Jacob knew she was worried about Toby. Here was their chance. Fred wasn't around, so they could tell their mom about their stowaway, and she'd figure out what to do. He opened his mouth to begin telling her, but "The End" flashed on the screen. The movie was finished, and was starting all over again.

Minerva sat down beside them with a whoosh and said, "Let's tell Fred that we've had enough of this museum and we're ready to leave now."

"Fine with me," their mom said.

They left the movie theatre and found the Finkles. They had discovered a whole additional part of the museum in an attached building with an enormous exhibit of farm equipment through the ages.

"Almost ready to leave?" Jacob's mom asked Fred.

"Leave? Oh no, my dear. Just look at this wonderful exhibit! I've never seen such a huge collection of farm machines. Look at this enormous threshing machine. They would feed the whole grain in right here, and it would spit out the chaff here in this funnel. Then they'd collect the grain over there. Isn't it all bloomin' fascinating?"

It would take forever to go through all the exhibits. Again, they had to get their money's worth, Fred insisted. He examined each and every machine in great detail, and commented on it with unbridled enthusiasm.

"Maybe we'll just wait for you in the cafeteria," Jacob's mom said after a while.

"What? Spend good money on that over-priced cafeteria food?' Fred said. "We have supplies of bread and peanut butter in the van, don't we? Perfectly adequate. We'll have a picnic lunch when we're finished looking around here."

Even Sam grew tired. "There aren't any dinosaurs here, Dad," he complained. "Not a single one."

Jacob could see that Minerva was becoming more and more agitated. Finally she said, "I'll just wait for you guys out in the car." And she left.

Everyone else was exhausted, dragging their feet and trailing along behind Fred.

Finally, Jacob's mom put her foot down. "You can stay as long as you like, my sweet, but the rest of us will be waiting for you in the cafeteria."

"Okay, okay, I'm coming," Fred said. He reluctantly left the exhibits and followed them outside.

After the museum's dim interior, the afternoon sunshine was dazzling. It was as if a bright blanket dropped over Jacob's head, muffling him with blinding light and heat. He pulled the brim of his cap down over his burning eyes. The lack of wind made the afternoon even hotter than usual. He wondered how Toby had fared in the car.

"What about lunch?" he asked his mom. "I thought we were going to eat in the cafeteria."

"We'll find a nice shady park for a picnic, maybe down by the river where it's cooler," his mom said. "Come and get some fruit to tide you over."

Jacob filled his pockets with oranges and bananas from the food box in the back of the van. "Can I take some of these granola bars too?"

"Yes, of course. And some for Minerva. She must be hungry too. Breakfast was such a long time ago."

In the Mini, Jacob found Toby was just waking up. Rivulets of perspiration trickled down her flushed cheeks and wisps of hair curled damply around her face. She or Minerva had put up towels on the windows to give her some shade. When he pulled the door open, she caught her breath and stared at him.

"Just Jacob," Minerva reassured her from the front seat. "Here's some cold water for you." She passed her the frosty bottle she had bought in the museum.

Toby swallowed. "Thank you and blessings." Her voice grated. "Surely am thirsty." She wiped the sweat from her forehead and poured water on the back of her neck.

"Here's some food too." Jacob gave her a banana and an orange.

The road out of Saskatoon didn't go beside the river so they didn't stop for a picnic after all. They kept driving south-east along an especially straight and quiet road, heading for the Manitoba border. With a fresh breeze blowing through the wide-open windows, the Mini soon cooled off. Mirages of lakes shimmered in the hot afternoon light on the road in front of them. The van was a fair ways ahead, barely visible on the horizon.

Since it was all so flat, Jacob begged Minerva to let him drive. "How am I ever going to learn if I don't get to practise? Here would be perfect."

"Okay, maybe this would be a good place to try." Minerva pulled the car to the side of the road.

The walkie-talkie beeped. Jacob picked it up.

"Mini here," he said into it.

"We just saw a sign for a community camp in Elkhorn, the next town, so we're stopping there for the night instead of trying to find a place for a picnic," his mom said.

So they had to postpone Jacob's driving lesson.

"Tomorrow," Minerva promised. "For sure."

The community camp was on a bare patch of land next to the highway at the edge of the village, but there was a big washroom that looked clean and the price was right, so they decided to stay. They pitched their tents as usual, near a picnic table.

"Get a load of this," Barney said to Jacob, who was pitching the tents while Minerva helped their mother with supper. Near their campsite were a couple of spindly trees less than two meters high. On each was a sign: "Please do not climb the trees."

"Ha," Jacob said. "That's a joke! Bet we could jump over them." He looked around the campsite. There were no other trees any higher than these in any direction on the flat prairie. What a contrast to the huge forests they'd come through in BC.

After supper, thick grey clouds rolled in and blocked out the sky, so they decided to get ready for bed early.

When Jacob went to get his toothbrush kit from the Mini, Minerva was in there whispering with Toby.

"You must be mistaken," Minerva was insisting. "No way could anyone know that you're hiding here in the Mini."

Toby was shaking her head. Her face was pale as paper. She looked scared.

"I told you, Brethren live all over. Spies are everywhere. My father could put out an alert and they could all be out looking for me and . . ."

"What's happening?" Jacob asked.

"Toby thinks she saw her father's van go by on the road a few minutes ago."

"And, and it stopped, right out there at the side the road." Toby's voice was high and trembling. "Like the people inside were staring right here, right at the Mini."

"That's crazy," Jacob said. "How could anyone follow us all the way from the Kootenays?"

"I don't know but it sure looked like my father's van. Maybe they're even camping in this campground tonight." Her voice ended with a scared tremor.

"I'll check if there are any other cars from BC here," Jacob said. "What did you say your dad's van looked like? What's its license number?"

"I don't know the license number but the van's big and beige. Lots of dust, dark windows. With a roof rack on top."

"What does your dad look like?"

"Um . . . black hair." Toby frowned as though she didn't like to picture him in her mind. "No beard or moustache."

Jacob nodded. As well as his toothbrush kit, he took out his soccer ball. He bounced it on the ground and kicked it along the dusty lane that went all around the campground.

A dozen or so other vehicles were parked at different camp-sites. Most were RVs, but there were a few people with tents as well. He checked all the license plates, but he didn't see a single other BC license.

The girl surely was paranoid. How could anyone possibly follow them here all the way from BC?

He went to the washroom and gave his teeth and face a good scrub, then went back to the Mini.

"No BC cars out there except us," he reported to Toby.

Minerva returned from the washroom. "I didn't see any BC cars either, Toby. Must have been just your imagination. You're safe here with us, you know. You shouldn't worry."

Chapter thirteen

B ut Toby did worry. Early the next morning, the clouds
had all blown away without releasing a single drop of
rain and now a pale blue sky arched overhead. Toby had
kept watch pretty well all through the night. As each vehicle swished by on the road, she held her breath. Expecting
that at any moment, her father and the elders would de-
scend upon the Mini and try to grab her, and she'd have to
escape into the fields, she kept her sandals strapped on to
be ready. But no one came.

Once morning arrived and she could see that no one was
around, she stretched her arms and legs that ached from

the cramped backseat. She rummaged through the pocket of her dress. Yes, the wad of paper with the all-important telephone number was still there.

A while later, when Minerva brought her rolled-up tent to stuff into the Mini, Toby asked her, "Is there a telephone around somewhere? I would surely like to call my aunt in Winnipeg to tell her I'm on my way."

"Saw one by the washrooms. No one's around at the moment, so you could call her now. I'll get some change from my wallet."

Toby followed her to the washrooms. The phone was gritty with prairie dust, but when she lifted the receiver, she heard a dial tone. She fed it some change from Minerva.

"Is this Charleen Wilson?" she asked when a woman's voice answered the phone.

"Who is this?" the woman asked. She sounded suspicious.

"It's Toby. You know. From home."

"Toby? Oh, my goodness! Little Toby. What a surprise! Where are you calling from?"

"Someplace near the Manitoba border. I've got a ride with some good friends, so I'll be in Winnipeg in a couple of days."

"Oh, that's so wonderful, dear!" Toby's aunt's warm voice reached out over the hum of the telephone lines and hugged her.

"I had to leave, to run away..."

"You did, eh? Can't say I'm surprised. How old are you now?"

"My birthday's next month, and I'll be turning fourteen, and . . . and . . ." Toby's voice faltered.

"Yes," her aunt said. "That's when they usually do it. Oh, Toby, I'm so happy you managed to get away from that place and that you're safe. Look, when you get closer to Winnipeg and you know exactly where you're going to be, call me and I'll come and pick you up. I'll give you my cell phone number in case you can't reach me at this one. It'll be so lovely to see you. Will you be all right until then?"

🚗 🚗 🚗

Jacob waited by the Mini, kicking his ball against the front tire, getting a good rhythm happening. Kick, bounce, kick, bounce, kick . . .

For once, Barney wasn't pestering him with his bad jokes. He was studying his *Giant Dinosaur Joke Book* for ammunition for later. Sam was already in the van playing with his dinosaur collection.

Fred was consulting the map with Jacob's mom. They had it spread out on the picnic table. Everyone had packed up and was ready to go.

"Where's your sister?" Fred asked Jacob.

"Gone to the washroom. Said she wouldn't be long."

"Looks like we could be in Brandon in a few hours, by noon or early afternoon, at the latest," Fred said. "Frank and Peggy said they'd hold lunch for us. Maybe we'll go on ahead. We'll stick to the quiet roads to avoid the Trans-

Canada Highway as long as possible. Too many bloomin' transport trucks. Just radio us on the walkie-talkie if there's a problem. You should be able to reach us since it has a ten kilometer range."

"Okay," Jacob nodded. He waved to his mom as their dusty van left the camp grounds. He dashed to the washroom. "Coast is clear. They're gone," he told his sister. "You guys can come now."

Minerva was waiting for Toby, who was talking on the phone.

Toby hung up and smiled at Jacob. He was amazed again at how a smile transformed her face. It was like looking at the sunniest and brightest day after weeks of dull grey weather. He found himself smiling back at her.

"My aunt said to call her when we got closer to Winnipeg so she'll know where and when to meet me. Oh, I can't wait to see her!" She hugged herself and skipped off to the Mini, her long braid bouncing on her back. "Come on, you guys," she called, climbing into the car. "What are you waiting for?"

The road leading out of the village, stretched ahead as straight as a meter stick. Not many vehicles were on the road, just a couple of grimy farm trucks. Jacob could see the Max away in the distance. He rested his head back on the seat and stared outside. There wasn't much to look at: a big bowl of pale sky with a distant frill of puffy clouds, the row of telephone poles laced with power lines sagging already in the early morning heat, and the dotted white line along the long narrow road stretching out to the horizon.

"What's your aunt like?" Minerva asked Toby after they'd been driving for a while.

"She's really nice. She was always friendly to me when I was a small child."

"Has she been in Winnipeg long?"

"She left the commune one night a couple of years ago. Took her five children. Dana, her daughter, is a couple of years older than me."

"Why'd she leave?"

"There was some kind of trouble with the elders."

"Trouble?"

"Something about her daughter," Toby said.

"Hey, Min. How about letting me take the wheel for a while?" Jacob said. "We're on a good straight road. Sure not much traffic. This might be my last chance."

"And no laurel hedges around here to trap you either," Minerva said, looking at the vast fields of grain swaying behind barbed wire fences on both sides of the road. "Okay, if you really want to. I guess it's now or never."

She pulled the car over and they switched places.

"Now, buddy-boy," she said in her teacher voice. "Remember to hold that clutch down when you change the gear into first. Then ease it up slowly while you give it some gas. Got it?"

"Yeah, yeah, yeah," he muttered. The steering wheel was

hot under his sweaty hands. "I got it."

He turned on the ignition with the key, pressed down on the clutch, pushed the gear lever forward, and then he pressed down on the gas. The motor raced.

"Not so much gas," Minerva instructed.

He eased back on the gas, but as he lifted his foot off the clutch, the car jolted forward.

"Easy does it," Minerva said, gripping the dashboard. "More gas now. More!"

"And ease just a bit off on the clutch," Toby piped up from the backseat. "That's always the trickiest part when I'm driving tractor."

Jacob lifted his foot from the clutch while pressing down harder on the gas. The motor raced. Then a loud bang! The car coasted to an abrupt stop and died.

"Now what?" Jacob said. "I was doing exactly what you guys said."

"Try the ignition again."

He did but nothing happened. The motor wouldn't start.

"Sounded like a tire blowing out," Toby said.

"If it was a tire, the motor should still work. But let's check," Minerva said.

They got out and looked. All the tires appeared normal. Dusty and dirty, but normal.

"Must be something in the motor," Minerva said, raising the hood and staring inside. "Bit of steam in here, but everything looks fine to me."

Jacob had no idea what to look for under the hood, and he suspected that Minerva didn't either.

"We better call Mom on the walkie-talkie," he said. By now the van was just a speck on the horizon.

The only traffic was a farm truck with a very wide load of hay coming up behind them. A farmer stuck his head out of the truck window. "Move that friggin' toy out of the way," he shouted. "What do you think this is? A playground?"

"So where's that good old prairie hospitality we've heard about?" Jacob said.

"Guy must be having a bad day," Minerva said.

"Maybe a bad life," Jacob said. "Come on. Let's push the car off the road."

"I'll steer while you two push," Toby said, climbing onto the driver's seat.

Jacob leaned against the dusty car's rear. Minerva grunted while she pushed beside him. Once they got it moving, the car was surprisingly easy to push off the road.

As the big farm truck trundled past, the farmer shook his fist at them. "Blasted city slickers! Think you own this friggin' road, or what!"

"Don't know what his problem is," Jacob said, reaching for the walkie-talkie on the dashboard. "I'll call Mom now before they get too far away."

At first he couldn't get through, but finally there was a crackle and he heard Barney's voice. "Max here," he said. "Come in, Min. Where are you guys? We can't see you."

"Car trouble," Jacob said. "About half an hour out of town. We need help."

He heard Barney tell his dad. "Okay," he said. "We're turning around. We're on our way. Big Max to the rescue! Say, while I have you on the line, what did the little dino say to the big dino?"

"Barney! This is no time for riddles." Jacob switched off the walkie-talkie and slapped it back on the dashboard. "Can you believe that guy?"

"Could be they'll have to tow the car to a garage to have it checked out," Minerva told Toby.

"Better let me out before they catch me," Toby said.

"You know, I still think we should tell Mom about you," Jacob said. But he moved away from the door so she could get out. "She'd know exactly what to do."

A flush of anger coloured Toby's cheeks. "Like call the police who will then call my father? I already told you what would happen to me then. It's just a day or two more and I'll be off your hands."

"No, it's not that . . ."

In the distance, the dark blue van approached.

Toby panicked. "Where can I hide?" She pulled the black T-shirt down over her legs nervously. "There aren't even any bushes around here." She looked up the road and down. The only bump on the horizon was a big rock on the other side of a shallow ditch beside the barbed-wire fence. Toby dashed towards the rock and leapt into the ditch beside it to hide among the long grass and reeds.

"If you keep your head down, no one will notice you from the road," Minerva called to her.

The Max pulled up in front of the Mini in a cloud of dust.

Fred climbed out. "So what's seems to be the problem?"

"There was a bang and now it just won't start," Minerva told him.

Jacob was grateful she didn't tell him that he had been driving when it happened. That it was probably all his fault.

Fred got in and tried the ignition. When nothing happened, he stared under the hood at the motor. He wiggled a few hoses and lines. "Festeration!" he said. "These little motors are impossible to service. Can't see anything obvious. We'll have to have it towed to a ruddy service station."

"There was a service station in Elkhorn where we camped last night. Maybe thirty or forty kilometers back," Jacob's mom said, consulting the map. "I think it's the closest one. It's quite a ways to the next town. You two want to wait with the car, or come with us?"

"I'll wait here," Minerva said.

"Me too," Jacob said. Being squashed into the crowded backseat between the Finkle brothers was something he wanted to put off as long as possible.

When the Max was out of sight, Toby crawled out of the ditch.

"You guys want an orange?" Jacob asked, pawing through his pack.

They sat at the edge of the road peeling oranges and sucking their tangy sweetness. Every time they spotted a vehicle on the horizon, Toby dived back to hide in the ditch.

"You're as jumpy as a frog in a frying pan," Jacob said. "That's just another dusty old farm truck."

"Can't be too careful," she said.

Minerva rummaged around in the back of the Mini. "Here's a tarp you can sit on until we get back," she told Toby. "And a magazine in case you get bored."

"And here are a couple of granola bars," Jacob said, tossing them to her.

"You two are so blessedly kind to me," she said. She had flipped the magazine open before they could blink. "My heavens! All about different musical groups."

"Do you have a favourite band?" Minerva asked her, spreading the dark green tarp in the short grass at the side of the road and lounging on it.

"I don't know any bands. At home, we aren't allowed to read magazines or listen to radio or watch television. The elders told us that everything on radio and television is evil and wicked. And I got into big trouble for reading a book I found."

"Do you really believe that, Toby? That everything in books and on the radio and TV is wicked?"

"That's what the elders say." Toby shrugged. She looked around as if she was half expecting someone else was listening. "Know what, Minerva?" she said in a low voice, sitting beside her on the tarp. "I'm beginning to think that not everything the elders say is true. Like, how could it be right that the Brethren will be the only people who will be saved on Judgment Day? I bet there are many good people all over the world and they should go straight to paradise too. Also, the leaders keep predicting the end of the world is coming but it never happens."

"Sounds like a scam to me," Jacob grunted.

"And they say that girls can't be friends with people just because they're boys," Toby went on. "My oldest brother, Johnnie, we were really good friends, but he was sent off to work on a cattle ranch somewhere in Utah, and he didn't even want to go. He wanted to study to be a doctor when he grew up, but the leader said that education was wicked and Johnnie had to quit school after grade six, even though he was smart and the best student in his class. Anyway, before he left, he said he would write me, but I never got a single letter from him. Not even a postcard."

Minerva shook her head. "I agree with you. Sounds like those old guys are telling you a pack of lies."

"And I really don't think it's fair that girls are sent off to marry old men even when they don't want to," Toby went on.

"Marry an old man? Yuck! I'd hate to do that," Minerva said, shivering. "Don't want to even think about it."

Toby shrugged, and flipped through the magazine.

"Toby," Minerva said, touching her arm. "Is that it? Is that really why you had to run away? Because they were forcing you to marry some old guy?"

Toby bit her lip. She looked away. "It . . . it isn't just any old guy," she blurted out. "It's this old man in Texas, he's a prophet, and, and I've heard some really creepy things about him and, and . . ."

"But why you?"

"My father said I was the chosen one. The prophet wants me because I'm blond, and I'm turning fourteen, and, and . . . They all said I should be happy to be set apart and be the chosen one." Her eyes flooded with tears.

"Oh, Toby! I can't imagine anything worse than being forced to marry a creepy old man."

"So that's why you ran away?" Jacob asked.

Toby sniffed and rubbed her nose. "They planned to send me off in a few weeks. The day before my birthday in September."

Minerva nodded. "I'm glad you managed to escape."

Toby flipped through the magazine and didn't say anything for a while.

Jacob bounced his ball on his knee. His stomach wrenched at the thought of an old man marrying this kid. He agreed with Minerva. It was mega-creepy. The girl was even younger than he was. He had so many questions in his head, but he couldn't think of how to ask them.

Toby cleared her throat. "So who is your favorite musical group?" she asked. She sounded as if she was trying to make her voice normal.

"I think I like the Black Eyed Peas best now," Minerva

said. "Their music really rocks. I think there's a photo of them in there."

"Show me." Toby gave her the magazine and Minerva flipped to a full-paged photo of the band.

"You look a lot like that one, don't you think?" Toby smiled at Jacob. "What's his name? Michael. Look. He's got hair like you do. Sort of ringlets."

"They're dreadlocks," Jacob said, twirling one of his front locks around his fingers.

"There's another thing the elders say that I can't believe," Toby said.

"What's that?" Minerva asked.

"Um, it's about people who aren't white. They say that all people who aren't white are inferior. Devil's spawn, they call them. They could never be saved and enter the gates of paradise because they are not as good as white people."

"Really?" Minerva pulled back from her. "So what do you think?"

"I had never met any non-white people before you and Jacob in my whole entire life. So I didn't know what to think. But now I know for sure, the elders got it all completely wrong. I've never met two people so nice and good as you two."

"Sounds to me like you've been living with a bunch of really ignorant and stupid people," Jacob snorted.

"They're not all bad," Toby said, coming quickly to their defence.

"Yeah, sure. They're a bunch of real nice people," Jacob said, sarcastically. He turned his back on her. He hated it when people said things like that. That non-white people weren't as good as white people. It made him restless and furious. Anger throbbed at his temples and he clenched his teeth. He got up and dribbled his soccer ball down the road's gravel edge. He kicked it so hard against the big rock, it bounced away into the tall reeds in the ditch. He chased it down and kicked it hard again. And again, and again.

It wasn't long before they spotted the Max on the horizon, coming towards them. A tow truck was right behind them.

Toby dived into the ditch again, taking along the tarp and magazine this time.

Just before the van arrived, Minerva hissed to her, "Shouldn't take that long to fix the car. Maybe an hour or two. Just sit tight. We'll be back for you soon. I promise."

Jacob clutched his ball and stared back at Toby. His stomach was still churning. Why should he care about a member of a bunch of racists?

On the other hand, she did say that she didn't believe everything the elders said. Still, it made him furious that there were such prejudiced people around.

Chapter fourteen

"Well, there's bad news and there's good news," Fred said at the service station, as he stared at the Mini that had been towed in.

"Okay, so what's the bad news?" Jacob's mom asked.

"The bad news is that although it's just the drive-belt pulley, the main bolt that holds the pulley onto the drive shaft is missing and they don't have one the right size here at the station, so they have to send someone to pick one up in the next town. That means the car won't be ready for a couple of hours."

Minerva looked at Jacob with raised eyebrows. He knew

she was worried about Toby. He didn't know what to think. Toby's remark about non-white people being "devil's spawn" and inferior to white people was still echoing inside his head. Even though she said she didn't agree with the elders, her remarks still stung.

"And the good news?" his mother asked.

"Behind the service station is a museum with an excellent collection of historical farm equipment and hunting weapons! Isn't that great!"

Everyone groaned.

The museum did have a superb solid concrete wall for Jacob to kick his soccer ball against, so it wasn't all bad. But they had to wait so long for the man from the garage to return, that Jacob even got tired of kicking his ball. Finally he saw the tow truck pulling into the service station.

"Tow truck's back," he called into the dim interior of the museum.

"Sorry, sir," the garage man said to Fred. "Roy at the Fleetwood station doesn't have the right size bolt you need for the Mini. It takes a real obscure size, that little guy does. But that's European cars for you."

"So what can we do?" Fred asked.

"I can get a bunch of different sizes sent over from Regina. But they won't get here until late tonight. Looks like your Mini won't be ready to roll until tomorrow."

Fred nodded. "All's not lost," he told the family. "We're not that far from Frank's in Brandon. We'll go and spend the night with him and come back here tomorrow. We wanted to visit with him and Peggy anyway."

So they all had to squash back into the van, the four kids jammed into the backseat.

"What about um, you know?" Jacob hissed to Minerva.

"What about what?" Barney asked, turning his flappy ears toward them.

"Oh, nothing," Jacob said, shrugging.

"We can't do anything about it right now," Minerva hissed back.

"What are you guys talking about?" Barney persisted.

"Hey, you ever hear about how a tyrannosaurus got rich?" Jacob said.

"No, how?" Barney asked.

"He charged everyone he saw."

"Hey, Jay. That's a really good one. Just a sec, while I get it down in my notebook." Barney jabbed his sharp elbow into Jacob's side as he rummaged around in his pack for his notebook.

Jacob sighed. Uncle Frank's place couldn't be that far. He leaned back in the seat and shut his eyes.

After a while, Minerva hissed in his ear. "Jay." She moved her head to point to the big rock at the field's edge.

He knew that was where Toby would be hiding in the ditch. What could they do about it? Not a thing. He strained to catch a glimpse of her as they passed the big rock. But he didn't see her. Maybe she was long gone by now, he thought.

Maybe she'd found a ride with someone else. Maybe some-one not good. Maybe someone from the commune had found her and tried to grab her and drag her back home and she escaped and ran into the fields . . . Maybe she was lying out there in the fields somewhere, dead. And it was all their fault . . . Jacob's heart pounded in his ears.

Barney and Sam looked at him, their eyebrows raised suspiciously, but they didn't say anything.

Chapter fifteen

The hot day stretched out. Toby lay on her stomach in the nest she had made of the tarp and some reeds in the ditch and read Minerva's magazine, turning the pages slowly, savouring every detail of the colourful photos and the fascinating articles about musicians and their friends and families. Some of them were dressed in strange and colourful clothing, but they didn't really look wicked or evil.

Then she heard what she thought was a dog barking quite close by, three loud barks. She raised her head, puzzled. There was no dog around that she could see. Maybe it was in the long grain in the fields. The only movement was from the wind, a strong and constant wind. Good, because it kept the pesky mosquitoes at bay. The dog barked again. Toby saw what it was and laughed. A big scruffy raven was hopping in the gravel at the road's edge. It whistled, hopping towards her with springy steps. She crawled out of the ditch, and as she approached the bird, it barked like a dog again and hopped a few meters away.

"Now, now, you old thing. I don't have anything much to feed you anyway." Her stomach grumbled, reminding her how hungry she was. She dug one of the granola bars Jacob had given her out of her pocket. She tore off the wrapping and bit into it hungrily. The raven hopped closer and whistled again. He cocked his head and stared at her with a hungry black eye.

"Fine. Here's a bit for you." She broke off a piece and held it out to him. He hopped closer, and closer. When he was about a meter away, he stopped. He wouldn't come any closer, no matter how much she coaxed, so she gently tossed the morsel of food to him. Before it hit the ground, he swooped over, grabbed it in his big curved black beak and crunched it down.

"Most wholesome, yes?" She took another bite. "Yum!" The granola bar was the most delicious thing she'd had all day. She wanted to eat it slowly, let each morsel melt in her mouth before swallowing it, but she was much too hungry.

The bird seemed to know that she didn't have any more food to share. It hopped away to scour the road's edge for more lunch while she gobbled up the rest of the bar and ripped open the second one. No point saving it. Minerva would be back for her soon. She had said it would be a couple hours at most, and at least one hour must have passed already. She crunched down the second bar and took a long drink from the water bottle, draining it. Now all she had left to eat was an orange. She would keep that until later.

Several vehicles had gone by and, as each one approached, she had hunkered down in the reeds in the ditch until it was out of sight. She was not taking any chances.

Now another vehicle approached. It was coming from the direction of the village. And, yes! It was a dark blue van with a yellow kayak on the roof. Minerva and Jacob's family. As it swished by, she could see several people inside. She thought she caught a glimpse of Jacob's anxious face in the back window, staring out at her.

So Minerva must be in the Mini right behind. Won't be long now. Her eyes on the horizon, Toby waited, and waited some more. Several other vehicles went by, but no Mini. She was sure of it. That little red car was unique here on the prairies, and she certainly would not have missed it if it had gone by without stopping.

What could have happened? Minerva had promised they would return for her. Toby waited some more. The sun was hot, blazing down on her head. She jammed Minerva's sun hat down over her hair and burrowed under the tarp for shade. That was a bit cooler. She opened the magazine again. There was nothing to do but wait.

An ad in the magazine for laundry detergent featured

clothes hanging on a clothesline. It reminded her of the evening after supper a few months ago, when she and Zelda were working together, gathering the washing from the clothesline. Zelda was one of the oldest of her father's many sister-wives.

"You will be marrying in the fall," Zelda had told her.

Toby had buried her face in the sweet-smelling clothes. She didn't want to get married in the fall. She didn't want to get married ever. Especially to some stranger. But how could she avoid it? She had made a solemn promise of obedience to God and to the community.

Then when Bertha had caught Toby reading in the night a few weeks ago, her father had quickly arranged to send her away to a commune in Texas so that on her fourteenth birthday, she would become the prophet's twenty-fifth wife. She had heard rumours of strange activities at the Texas commune. And that the old man was cruel and forced his wives to do degrading things.

"Please, Father," she begged. "Please don't send me away."

He looked at her sternly. "You are the Chosen one, my daughter. You have been set apart and spoken for. When the prophet hears that I have sent you to him, he will understand my own devotion and obedience. And yours as well. And he will bestow blessings upon us and our whole community. When the hallowed union is made, it will be the happiest day of your life." He licked his wet lips, bent down and fondled a wisp of her hair.

Her stomach turned with revulsion but she didn't dare pull away from him. No point pleading with him. Her father had decided to send her away. And that, as far as he was concerned, was final.

At that moment, she decided something as well, that she must try to escape from the commune at the first opportunity.

She had no other choice.

🚗 🚗 🚗

After a few hours, the sun had moved low in the western prairie sky. The wind dropped to a hush. Bugs came out and formed a whining haze over Toby's head. She tried flapping them away with the magazine, but the movement only encouraged them, so she cowered under the tarp for protection.

Clouds gathered in the north, big puffy grey clouds and then a dark thunderhead came nearer. A sudden lightning flashed. A few seconds later, distant thunder rumbled. The darkening sky was slashed by another forked lightning. Toby counted slowly. One, two, three. A loud boom of thunder made the ground around her shudder.

"Three kilometers away," she muttered. At least the blessed wind had come up again and blown away the pesky mosquitoes.

She heard the van coming long before it reached her, so

she had plenty of time to duck low in the long grass in the ditch. She peeked through the reeds. The dusty beige van had darkened windows and a three-prong roof rack. And a BC license. It travelled slowly, crawling along as though the driver was searching the road's edge and the fields for something.

Or someone.

And Toby knew who that someone was.

Her heart pounded. She was sure the van was her father's! That meant Minerva and Jacob had been wrong. Her father really had been following her all along. And somehow he knew she had been hiding in the Mini.

Why else would the van be here on this quiet road?

He was just waiting for an opportunity to grab her and drag her back to the commune.

She held her breath, her muscles tensed, ready to escape into the fields if the van stopped. But it kept moving away slowly, and eventually its red rear lights faded into the dusk.

It started to rain. Big cold drops splashed on the plastic tarp. She hunkered down and pulled the tarp around herself, trying to stay dry, but water trickled onto her back and soon her T-shirt was soaked. She shivered and rocked back and forth, humming to keep herself company.

One thing for sure, she could not leave her little nest now, not with that beige van combing the countryside for her. She was much safer just staying put. If Minerva had said she would be back for her, then she would. She had to trust her.

She had no choice.

But maybe Jacob had managed to convince her not to come. She wasn't entirely sure about him. After she mentioned how people in her community viewed non-white people, he seemed angry with her. She agreed with him that the people on the commune were ignorant about such things, especially now that she'd had a chance to meet Minerva and Jacob. But somehow it bothered her when Jacob said bad things about her family. Especially when she thought of the friends she had left behind and would probably never see again, Sonia and Dora and Ellie. They just didn't know any better.

Anyway, she had to wait here until morning. If Minerva hadn't returned by then, she would decide what to do. She burrowed down into the reeds and listened to the rain pattering on the tarp. Eventually she fell into a fitful sleep.

Chapter sixteen

Jacob was just dozing off in the stuffy crowded backseat of the van when they finally reached Brandon. He was jammed up against the door and he was tired of sitting in the same position. He couldn't wait to get out and stretch his legs.

Fred turned the van onto a cool shady road lined with big leafy trees. "Here we are," he announced. "Uncle Frank and Auntie Peggy's house."

Jacob was the first one out of the van. He dropped his soccer ball to the ground and dribbled it down the sidewalk, working the kinks out of his back and his legs.

"Sorry we're so bloomin' late," Fred said as they all

crowded into the house. "We had car trouble."

The door had been opened by a man who could have been Fred's twin. "No problem at all. Come on in. Come on in, one and all. Welcome! Welcome! I bet you're all bloomin' exhausted."

Jacob soon discovered Frank Finkle was as talkative as Fred. Although they weren't actual twins, he and Fred looked a lot alike with their dark beards, and long hairy legs. And their loud English voices sounded exactly the same.

They made Jacob think about the twins in the Tintin books. Minerva grinned at him. She caught on too. Jacob expected them to say, "Billions of Blustering Bloomin' Blarney Stones!"

"And the lovely Rosalina," Uncle Frank said, kissing Jacob's mom's hand gallantly. "Haven't seen you since your wedding. Welcome, welcome, welcome."

He pulled Barney and Sam close in a rough bear hug. "Blimey, you two have grown! Won't be long and you'll be even taller than your dad here. And you two must be Minerva and Jacob. Bet you don't remember me at the wedding. It's all a haze for me too."

Jacob was afraid for a minute that they were going to be hugged and kissed as well, so he hung back. But Uncle Frank just shook his hand warmly, and did the same to Minerva.

"So come on in. You must be bloomin' starved to death. Peggy's made a big feast for you."

Auntie Peggy was friendly too. She was short and plump with blond hair, the complete opposite of the tall slim, knobby-kneed Uncle Frank. And she had prepared a mountain of food for them: bowls of thick tomato soup, platters of turkey and cheese sandwiches, a gigantic salad and gallons of lemonade. They all descended upon the meal and, for a full minute, no one said a word.

Jacob rubbed his full stomach. He thought about Toby. He didn't want to, but her thin, scratched face flashed into his head. She'll be starving out there in the fields. Yet what could he do about it? He reached for another delicious, home-made oatmeal chocolate chip cookie, but suddenly, he couldn't eat another bite.

"It's still early enough for a swim," Uncle Frank was saying. "We have a new park, Curran Park. It's on the outskirts of town and has a small man-made lake which provides a wonderful swimming place. How about it?"

It was hot and stuffy, so everyone agreed to go for a swim. After their late lunch, they gathered swimsuits and towels and drove to the outskirts of town in two cars. The man-made lake was like a pond with a sandy beach and clear water, refreshing in the muggy afternoon. It looked as if half the town was there, it was so crowded.

Jacob splashed past a bunch of little kids playing with inflatable toys close to the shore under the watchful eyes of their caretakers. When he got in deeper, he toppled into the water which covered his head like cool silk. He turned to float on his back and stare up at the blue sky streaked with clouds. This was fabulous!

Minerva splashed his face, and he came up sputtering. "Hey, no fair," he laughed, splashing her back. Barney got into the act and soon they were both splashing her and she was squealing and trying to escape. Everyone was having so much fun fooling around in the water they didn't notice a thick bank of dark clouds drifting across the sky from the northern horizon.

The air was split by a sudden clap of thunder so loud, it rattled Jacob's eardrums. He blinked water out of his eyes. A dark grey cloud had rolled in to obscure the sun.

"Attention everyone!" An urgent announcement crackled over some speakers. "Everyone must get out of the water! Immediately. Hurry! There's danger of an electrical storm. Hurry! Everyone out of the water now. This is an emergency!"

Uncle Frank swam over to them with long hurried strokes and yelled, "We've got to get out right now! You might get struck by bloomin' lightning in the water when there's an electrical storm like this."

Jacob shrugged at Minerva's questioning look, but he followed everyone out of the water. Everyone except Sam.

Sam was bobbing around in the long reeds. Jacob knew he would be so involved in his game of playing dinosaurs, diving in and under the water, that he wouldn't be paying any attention to the announcement. He was in his own world.

A bright flash of lightning lit up the air and the ominous

rumble of thunder shook the ground. People shouted and scurried for the shelter of their cars or the overhanging roof of the washrooms.

Minerva shrieked and grabbed her towel. She headed for the washrooms but Jacob stopped her. "Min! Sam's still out there in the reeds."

"Oh, no! Where's Fred?"

They couldn't see Fred anywhere in the chaotic crowd. Another clap of thunder crashed around them. Jacob ducked under his towel.

"Sam! Have you seen Sam?" Fred ran to them, frantic. His hair was standing on end and his beard was all bushy.

"He's there. Out in the reeds." Jacob pointed. "Didn't hear the warning."

"Where?" Fred yelled. "Where is he?"

Jacob ran down to the water's edge, Fred on his heels. "There! See him?" He pointed to a glint of Sam's bobbing white back.

Fred lost no time. "Come on! We've got to get him!" he yelled. "He could get struck by lightning!" He grabbed an inflated boat from the beach, threw it into the waves and jumped on it. Jacob was right behind him.

Fred called out, "Sam! Sam!"

Jacob couldn't see the boy now. But he knew he must still be out there in the reeds. Jacob didn't have a paddle so he thrashed his hands in the water, which was now rough with whitecaps. He dug into the foam, paddling as hard and fast as he could. Fred knelt beside him and paddled frantically as well. The little boat bounced through the waves. As it bumped into the reeds, the air flashed with blinding light, followed immediately by crashing thunder.

Jacob ducked. His heart throbbed in his throat. Man! That lightning must be really close. He caught a glimpse of Sam's white back again in the reeds. "He's there! Over there!" he yelled, pointing.

Fred dived in and splashed to the boy. He grabbed him, and hauled him to the boat.

Jacob clung to a bunch of reeds to steady the boat in the wind and waves while Fred pushed Sam up. Sam stared at Jacob with huge scared eyes.

Jacob pulled him onto the raft beside him, muttering, "It's okay, kiddo. We'll get you back to shore. It's okay."

Again, jagged lightning slashed the sky. Thunder growled menacingly at them.

"Let's go," Fred shouted over the sound. He pushed the boat away from the reeds. "Back to shore. Now! Start paddling. I'll kick."

Jacob dug into the water and paddled like mad, Sam crouched beside him, shivering like a scared puppy. Blinding white flashes of lightning and crashes of thunder rolled around them.

Jacob paddled even harder.

He felt the raft surge ahead as Fred kicked up a frenzied spray. It was like being pushed by a motor boat going full blast.

Jacob held onto Sam's shivering back and tried to keep

the boat on course to shore. Finally, it bumped into the shallows. Jacob jumped off and pulled Sam through the water onto the beach. Fred was right behind them.

Fred folded Sam into a tight hug, patting his head. He was breathing hard.

So was Jacob. A big wave bounced against the boat and it started to drift, so he splashed back into the water and hauled the boat up onto the sand. The rain was coming down hard now, in big cold drops.

"You're okay?" Fred shouted to him.

Jacob nodded.

"Thanks, Jay," Fred said, his beard twitching into a smile. "You were a great help out there."

Jacob shook his head. "Didn't know anyone could push a boat through the water that fast."

His mom and Minerva rushed to them, babbling, "Are you okay? Are you okay?"

Jacob's mom wrapped a big towel around Sam and hugged him close. "We were so worried about you, Sammy, child. So worried."

Another flash of lightning forked through the rain, followed by an echoing rumble of thunder. Wind blew up the sand, stinging their legs.

"Make tracks to the car," Jacob shouted, grabbing a towel from Minerva.

They sprinted through the downpour to the vans where Barney was waiting anxiously with Uncle Frank and Auntie Peggy.

"There you are!" she said. "All soaked. You must be freezing. Let's go home and get some hot soup into you water fiends."

After hot showers and dry clothes, they all sat down to supper: a big pot of homemade soup, followed by juicy chicken burgers, and a big green salad with lettuce and tasty tomatoes, fresh from the garden.

Everyone was giddy with relief, talking all at once about the rescue.

"But why didn't you come out of the water when there was the announcement over the loudspeaker?" Auntie Peggy asked Sam.

He shrugged. "Just didn't hear it."

"Good thing your dad went in after you," Jacob's mom said.

"And Jacob too," Sam said, looking at him with shining eyes. "Jacob's a hero."

"No way," Jacob said. "It was your dad that rescued you. I just held you on the boat in case you fell in."

"I'm proud of both of you," his mom said. "You're both my heroes." She hugged and kissed Fred who was sitting beside her at the table.

"Blimey! I should be a hero every day," Fred said, grinning.

Everyone laughed. Funny how his mom kissing Fred

used to bother him a lot, Jacob thought. But now. Not at all.

"So who's for homemade rhubarb pie and ice cream to celebrate?" Auntie Peggy asked.

After supper, once the rain had stopped, the kids pitched their tents in the backyard, while Fred and Jacob's mom slept indoors in Marty's room. Marty was Uncle Frank and Auntie Peggy's son, who was studying chemistry in Toronto.

There wasn't enough level space in the backyard for three tents, so Minerva said to Jacob, "You can bunk with me tonight if you want. As long as you leave your smelly socks outside the tent."

"Smelly socks? My socks aren't smelly. They're clean today."

"Okay, your smelly shoes then."

"All right, all right," he muttered, pushing off his sneakers and crawling inside.

They spread out their sleeping bags, one along each side of the tent.

"That was some rescue out there in the lake this afternoon," Minerva said.

"I didn't do much," Jacob said. "Really. It was Fred. He was like a superhero out there. I didn't know he had it in him."

"When it's your own kid in danger, I guess that gives you super powers," Minerva said.

"Yeah, I guess." Jacob crawled into his sleeping bag and thought about their own dad. It was almost five years now since the fatal car accident. "If it had been one of us in danger, and our dad was around, I guess he would have come after us."

"Sure he would have," Minerva said. "You still miss him? I sure do."

"Yeah. But Mom's pretty happy with Fred, I guess."

A cold wind had picked up and was rattling the tent.

"Sure am worried about Toby," Minerva said. "She must be freezing out there in all this wind and rain."

"I'm worried too," Jacob said. "But look, the bottom line is she's really not our responsibility. Like I've said a million times, we should just tell Mom about her. She'll know what to do. I think this whole secret has gone on way long enough."

"And I say, we can't tell anyone. Toby doesn't want us to. And we promised her we wouldn't. At least I did. She's right that they would have to report her to the police, who would end up sending her back home. You know they would. And that would be the worst thing possible for her. Imagine being forced to marry some hideous old man and having to live with him for the rest of his life. What if he lived to a hundred? Imagine actually sleeping with him. Yuck! Doesn't it just make your stomach heave?"

"They're all just a bunch of bigoted racists anyway," Jacob muttered.

"Maybe some people in her community are racists, but Toby isn't. You know she's not. As she said, she'd just never in her whole life met anyone before us who wasn't white. If you're taught to be a racist from when you're a little kid, it's not surprising that after all those years of brainwashing, you end up that way."

"Can't stand such ignorant people. They make my blood boil."

"I think this whole experience has really opened Toby's eyes. And just because some people in her community are racist, doesn't mean they all are."

"Right," Jacob said sarcastically. "They're all as pure as the driven snow in that community. Especially those old guys that so-call 'marry' kids like her. I don't know who they think they're fooling." He punched a hollow into his pillow with his fist. "Yeah, okay. I won't tell anyone. You don't even know if she'll still be there tomorrow. How are you going to pick her up without Fred or Mom finding out?'

"Don't know. We'll think of something. We have to. I gave her my word." Minerva yawned and pulled her sleeping bag over her ears. She was soon snoring away.

Jacob was exhausted, but he tossed and turned in his sleeping bag far into the night. He couldn't shake the image out of his head, of those hungry blue eyes in the face of that skinny little kid who was lying in a ditch under a black and threatening sky.

Chapter seventeen

Toby woke in the night, cold and wet and hungry. She was so hungry she would have eaten almost anything. Her back ached with stiffness and so did her legs. The ground under her was wet. She shivered and stood up and stretched. The rain was long gone. A black moonless sky loomed overhead, the stars glittering brightly. She remembered what the prophet had said about the stars falling at the end of the world, which could happen at any moment, so she averted her gaze from them.

The road was quiet. No car lights in either direction. The only sounds were the hum and chirping of night insects.

And way off in the distance, the occasional three-note yelp of a coyote. And an answering call. As long as the animals kept their distance, she wouldn't worry about them. Even the mosquitoes weren't bothering her now. Probably too cold for them.

She crawled through the barbed-wire fence into the field of grain, scaring off a few early birds who squawked down at her as they flew away. She broke off a head of wheat and rubbed it between her palms, loosening the husk as she'd seen her uncles doing in the fields. She opened her hand and blew away the chaff, leaving a handful of tiny oval-shaped grains. She crushed them between her teeth, savoring the tiny nutty sweetness. She chewed until the grain formed a gummy paste and she swallowed it. Then she broke off another head of wheat and chewed it as well. Not much in the way of food but it was something.

The stars faded eventually and morning's first light glowed in the east. A bright dot of a vehicle's lights appeared in the distance. She ducked between two swaying rows of grain and lay flat, her cheek pressed into the wet earth. She would be really conspicuous from the road up here on the raised field. The vehicle approached. She caught her breath. It swished by without stopping. She waited until she couldn't hear it any longer. She got up and brushed off the bits of dried grass then slipped back through the barbed-wire and dashed down into the ditch again, back to her nest of reeds and tarp where she would be out of sight.

After her meager breakfast of raw grain, her throat and

mouth were dry as paper. She had eaten the orange from Jacob a long time ago. Minerva's water bottle was empty, but there was a trickle of water in the ditch as a result of last night's rain. Should she chance a drink? It might be contaminated. She stared down for a while at the water running between the pebbles. It looked clean. She dipped the water bottle in, filling it. Then she took a cautious sip of the cold water. It tasted so blessedly sweet and delicious that she had a long drink and rinsed out her mouth. That was better. Now what should she do?

She looked up and down the road again. She couldn't be that far from Winnipeg, a few hundred kilometers maybe. Should she try hitching a ride? Auntie Charleen was expecting her in a few days.

She smiled when she thought of her. Auntie Charleen was a big strong woman, and outspoken. If she didn't like something, you were sure to hear about it. But she had always been friendly and nice to Toby, even when she was a really little kid.

It had caused a huge scandal a few years ago when her aunt had fled from the commune, sneaking off in the night in her car, taking along her five children. They heard that she had gone east to Winnipeg where she had found a big house to live in. Then it was as though she and her children had totally disappeared or died, because no one mentioned her or her children's names ever again. It was as though they had never even existed.

Toby was lucky to have her phone number. She got it from

the teacher who came to their commune sometimes when the elders had their weekly visit into town. The teacher taught reading and writing to whoever wanted to learn. Toby was her most enthusiastic student.

She stretched out and sighed. She remembered the elaborate ceremony a couple of years ago when she and her three half-brothers, Thad, Travis and Thomas, had turned twelve. They were known as "the Ts" because they had all been born in the same year. The whole community and even some visitors from sister communes in the States had come to the ceremony. The community hall had been decorated with sweet-smelling flowers and cedar bows and flickering candles, and they sang hymns. Toby and her half brothers had dressed in long flowing white gowns and they had walked slowly to the front of the hall where they solemnly promised to uphold the laws of the elders and be obedient and loyal servants now and for the rest of their lives.

Toby sighed again. She surely had failed in that. Her running away was disobedience and a grievous sin. She was wicked, wicked, wicked. And according to the teachings, she would be condemned to burn in the abyss of hell forever. But what else could she do? She simply could not marry that old man. She would rather die first.

She stared down the dusty road. It looked as though Minerva wasn't coming back after all. Something must have happened. So now maybe she would have to try getting a ride from someone else. When a car was approaching from the right direction, she would make sure it wasn't her father's beige van. Then she would scramble up onto the side of the road and wave the car down. Someone was bound to stop. They would see that she was desperate for a lift. Maybe she would even find someone on their way to Winnipeg. Someone who could take her all the way there.

But what if it was someone connected to their commune? One of the brethren who had been told that she had escaped and that her father was out searching for her? She knew that all over the country there were spies who would report to her father and the elders.

Or what if it was some terrible person, a killer on the lookout for young girls like her? She had heard about people like that.

On the other hand, she couldn't just lie in this ditch starving to death, waiting for someone to rescue her, someone who wasn't coming back. She had to do something.

A car was approaching from the east. She ducked down into the weeds as usual and peered out. The car was a dark blue van with a yellow kayak strapped to the roof. And yes! The license was Beautiful British Columbia! Probably Minerva's family's van on its way back to the village to collect the Mini. Maybe it had taken longer to repair it than they expected.

Great! Maybe Minerva hadn't abandoned her after all. Now all she had to do was wait a little longer until Minerva came back with the repaired Mini.

After what seemed to her to be hours, but maybe wasn't, she saw a Mini coming towards her from the village. Her heart leaped. It must be Minerva's Mini. The little red car was unmistakable. Toby held her breath. Her muscles tensed. She was ready to leap up and rush into the safety of its backseat under Minerva's cozy quilt.

But the car didn't stop! It just sped on by. In fact, it didn't even look like Minerva was driving. Who else could it be?

Were they abandoning her here, in the middle of the prairies?

She was starving, and she was alone.

Totally alone.

Hunger and loneliness gnawed at her insides. Tears clouded her eyes.

Now what? Now what could she do?

Chapter eighteen

Earlier that same morning at the breakfast table in Brandon, Fred and Uncle Frank were talking about going to pick up the Mini.

Minerva said, "I'd like to come along as well, if that's okay."

"Certainly," Fred said. "Especially since the Mini is your car now. The more you learn about it, the better."

Jacob felt Minerva kick his shin under the table. He shrugged at her. He was still groggy from the restless night in the tent worrying about Toby.

"How about you, Jay? Want to come along for the ride?"

she asked, nodding at him. She was making two slices of toast into a thick peanut butter sandwich. She wrapped it in her paper napkin and slipped it to her lap, out of sight. He knew right away who that sandwich was for.

"So?" she prodded him.

He could see that she really wanted him to come. "Okay, I guess. I can sleep on the way there."

After breakfast, they carried their cereal bowls into the kitchen. Auntie Peggy was loading the dishwasher.

"Thank you," she said, smiling her big friendly smile at them. "How about taking a snack for on the way to Elkhorn? You probably won't be back until after two for lunch and you'll be starving by then." She wrapped chocolate chip cookies, grapes and bananas and dropped the food into a yellow plastic Super Store bag. "There. That should hold you until you get back. You don't want to spoil your appetite for lunch. Your mom and I will be cooking up a storm this morning."

"Sounds good," Jacob said, taking the bag. "Thanks." He followed Minerva outside to their tent.

"So tell me why I have to come with you?" he asked Minerva in the tent, as they rummaged around for their toothbrushes.

"We've got to figure out how to pick up Toby. I might need your help."

Although he'd tossed and turned half the night worrying about her, he was definitely not enthusiastic about hiding her in the back of the Mini again.

"Come on, Jay," Minerva said. "We got her this far. Winnipeg's only a few hundred kilometers more. Then she'll be safe with her aunt. We can't leave her stranded in the middle of the prairies where she doesn't know anyone."

"So how are you going to pick her up without the Bobbsey twins figuring it out?"

"Don't know yet, but we'll think of something. We have to."

It was a three-hour drive back to the village of Elkhorn. Jacob stretched out on the luxurious backseat of the van and snoozed most of the way. One thing about this car, it was sure a lot roomier than the cramped Mini.

Fred and Uncle Frank were engaged in a lively conversation about global warming or conservation or something. Their voices lulled Jacob into a stupor.

Minerva stared out the window, plugged into her I-Pod. After they'd been on the road for a couple of hours, she elbowed him awake. "There," she hissed, "by that big rock. That's where we left her."

He forced his eyes open to stare out at the fields of swaying grain. No one was in sight. Not even a skinny blond kid.

At the garage, the Mini was ready and waiting for them in front, its red coat glistening. The guys at the station had given it a much-needed wash.

Minerva stroked its roof as if it were her favourite pet cat.

"Surely would fancy driving that baby. Would you mind?" Uncle Frank asked her. "It's been years since I've actually been behind the wheel of a Mini. Why, the last time was way back when I was at university. One of my friends had one and we would take it out into the country on the weekend for excursions or to go on climbing trips. Amazing how bloomin' much you can cram into one of those. Why, I remember one trip when we packed it full of . . ."

A volcano of words poured over them. Jacob wondered if it were possible that Uncle Frank talked even more than Fred?

"Sure, I guess," Minerva said when he stopped to catch his breath.

When he turned away to talk to Fred, Jacob asked her, "So what's the plan?"

They moved to the other side of the van where she said in a low voice, "The only thing I can think of is that when we get to the big rock, I could tell Fred that he has to stop because I have to go to the bathroom urgently. And when he stops, I'll sneak Toby into the van."

"No way that would work. Besides, she's probably long gone by now."

"I think she'll still be there. I did promise that we'd be back for her, remember? Sure hope nothing's happened to her."

Jacob shook his head. "If she is still in that ditch, there's no way you could sneak her into the van without Fred noticing."

"Then it'll be up to you to distract Fred so I can get her in safely."

"How am I going to do that?"

"I don't know. You'll have to think of something."

On their way back to Brandon, Jacob had to sit up front with Fred while Minerva had the whole backseat to herself. Fred decided that it would be better if they followed the Mini this time so if it had problems again, they would see it right away.

After they had been on the road for about half an hour, Minerva said, "Would you mind stopping, Fred? I have to go to the bathroom. Up by that big rock looks like a good spot."

"Why didn't you use the washrooms at the garage?"

"I didn't have to go then. But I really, really have to go now." Her voice rose to a desperate tone. "Please!"

Jacob had to put his hand up to cover his grin. Minerva sure could act.

"Okay, okay. I didn't want to lose sight of the Mini in case Frank has a problem."

"He'd call us on the walkie-talkie," Jacob pointed out.

Fred pulled the van over to the road's edge and stopped not far from the big rock. Minerva poked Jacob's shoulder to remind him about distracting Fred. Then she slid open the door and hopped out.

"Um . . ." Jacob had to think fast. What would Fred be interested in around here? There was nothing out there except the waving fields of grain. "Have you ever examined that grain up close?" he asked Fred.

"No. Have you?"

Jacob shook his head. "I think the grain around here must be almost ready to harvest now, don't you? Wonder what it looks like when it's all ripe."

"We could check it out in the field on the other side of the road," Fred said.

"Sure. Let's." Grinning to himself, Jacob followed Fred across the road and into the field. You could always count on Fred to be interested in anything new. Jacob picked up a heavy head of grain. "Wonder what this is," he said. "Wheat, maybe? Or rye?" He glanced over Fred's shoulder. Minerva was hurrying back toward the van. A little kid in a black T-shirt was following her. Toby! He felt a rush of relief. She was still there! And she was safe!

"Hmm," Fred said, stripping off the husk of the grain. "This must be the stuff they get rid of when it goes through the threshing machine. But I guess we'd better be on our way. Your sister must be ready by now." He turned to go back to the van.

Jacob couldn't think of anything else to say to keep Fred in the field.

Fred glanced across the road and a puzzled look crossed his face. "There seems to be someone with Minerva."

Oh no! He'd spotted Toby. Now what?

Jacob trailed after him back to the van.

"Who did you find there, Minerva?" Fred asked. "Some-one lost?"

"Oh, hi. Ah, yes. This is um, Toby. She's hitching a ride and I thought we could, um . . . give her a lift into Brandon. If that's okay with you?"

"Funny," Fred said. "I didn't see her when we stopped."

"No, she was back near that rock."

"So where are your folks, Toby?" Fred asked.

"They'll be waiting for her in Brandon. Right, Toby?"

"In Brandon. Yes," Toby said. Her voice was gritty, as if she hadn't spoken for awhile. Her pale face was streaked with dirt and although her blond hair was still in a braid, long strands had escaped and were flying around her face. She pulled them back.

Minerva pushed her into the van's backseat. "They said for her to meet them at — um . . ." She saw the yellow plastic Super Store grocery bag of fruit. "The Super Store in Brandon."

"But why aren't you with them now?" Fred wanted to know.

"Um, well, um . . ." Toby gave Minerva a wild look. Help me, she seemed to say.

"Guess we better get going," Jacob said. "Uncle Frank must be miles ahead now."

"You're right," Fred said. "Okay, buckle up, everyone."

Minerva gave Toby a water bottle which she emptied in seconds. She tucked into Minerva's peanut butter sandwich, stuffing it into her mouth as though she were trying to get the whole thing down at once. Then she attacked a banana

and the grapes the same way. Jacob's stomach grumbled. He
was hungry, but she probably hadn't eaten much for a couple of days. He handed her his banana. She needed it more
than he did.

"Thanks," she muttered, her mouth full.

Minerva moistened a paper towel from another water
bottle and gave it to Toby. She washed the streaks of dirt
from her face and neck. They were involved in a hushed
conversation. Jacob knew they were planning what to do
after dropping her off in Brandon. He turned on the radio
so Fred wouldn't overhear them.

A few kilometers down the road, the walkie-talkie beeped
on the dash board. Jacob picked it up. "Hello? Max here."

"Where are you? Can't see you in my rear view mirror,"
Uncle Frank's voice came in. "Everything okay?"

"Everything's fine," Jacob said. "We stopped for a few
minutes but we're on our way now. Say, where's the Super
Store in Brandon?"

"A few blocks south of our place on 9th and Victoria
Avenue. You can't miss it."

"Roger and out."

When they finally got to Brandon, Fred found the big
Super Store supermarket easily. He drove into the crowded
parking lot.

"These places are always so bloomin' busy," he grumbled,
but he eventually found a parking spot quite far from the
entrance. "So this is where you are meeting your folks,
Toby?" he asked.

"Yes, this is it," she said. She looked a little better now that she'd had something to eat and drink, and had washed her face and tidied her hair. "Thank you, sir, very much for the ride."

"Just a minute. Maybe we should wait until you see your folks."

"Oh no," she said. "I'll find them. Not a problem. I meet them here at the Super Store all the time. Thank you again. And bless you." She smiled her dazzling smile at Fred and quickly got out of the car. She hurried away to become lost in the supermarket crowd.

"I don't like leaving such a little girl all alone though," Fred said.

"She said she meets her folks here all the time," Jacob told him.

"True." Fred shook his head and stared after her. "Strange but I'm sure I've seen that little girl before. Haven't you two?"

"Us? Oh no," Jacob lied. "I've never seen her before. Ever." He kicked the dash board. He hated lying.

Minerva was already plugged into her I-Pod, listening to her music, so she was no help.

"Sure am starving," Jacob said. "Wonder what treats Mom and Auntie Peggy have made for lunch. She's a terrific cook, isn't she?"

"You're right. Wonder if there's any of that delicious rhubarb pie left from last night," Fred said. "Let's go and find out."

Late in the night, Jacob was awoken by a scratching at the door flap of the tent. He knew right away without even checking who it was. Toby.

"Min," he whispered, nudging his sister in her sleeping bag with his toe. "She's here."

Minerva just snored back at him so he had to zip open the flap himself. Sure enough, it was Toby. Her big dark eyes were staring out of her pale face.

"Minerva's out cold," he told her. "Usually takes a bomb to wake her."

"Can I come in?" Toby was shivering. She had pulled the black T-shirt down over her knees.

"Sure. I guess."

She crawled into the tent and crouched in the entrance. It was so dark that he couldn't see her very well, but he could smell her. She needed a good shower and a change of clothes. She smelled of underarm sweat, and something else. Something sweeter. Clover? Wild grain?

"How did you find us?" he asked.

"Minerva told me to look in the telephone book at the Super Store so I did. Only one Finkle in all of Brandon. Not that common a name."

"Guess you're right."

"And I knew this was your tent. Couldn't mistake Minerva's snoring anywhere. Had to wait until all the lights in the house were out though. Those people surely stay up late. Do you have any food? I'm starving." She shivered again.

"I could use a snack myself. Stay here and I'll go in and see what I can find. And I'll try to get a blanket or something for you. Meanwhile, use my sleeping bag until I get back."

Auntie Peggy had left a night light on in the hallway so they could find their way to the bathroom if they needed it. The light illuminated the kitchen enough so he could see the fridge. He opened it. It was filled with goodies. He quickly collected a bowl of leftover stew, a hunk of cheese and a couple of apples and quietly slid back outside.

"Sorry, the stew's not hot." He gave Toby the bowl. She had pulled his sleeping bag around her shoulders.

"Doesn't matter." She snapped off the plastic lid, tilted the bowl into her mouth and slurped and chewed and swallowed until the bowl was empty. Then she ran her fingers around the edge to catch the last bit of gravy. She smacked her lips. "Glory be. That must be the best meal I have had since I don't know when. What else do you have?"

He was munching on an apple. "Here's an apple for you. And this cheese."

"Yum." She made short work of that as well. "Bless you."

A cold breeze fanned his back. "Oh, I forgot a blanket for you. Look, you may as well get into the Mini and sleep there for the night. I think Minerva's quilt's still in the backseat."

"I already tried to get in but the doors are locked. Do you have the key?"

"Min usually keeps it in her toothbrush kit." He felt

around for the key in Minerva's kit. "Drat. Not here. Oh, I remember. Uncle Frank was driving the car today so he probably put the key on their key rack by the back door. I'll check." He snuck back into the house. Yes, the Mini key with its braided leather key ring was on the rack by the back door.

He brought it back and soon Toby was on her way.

"Thanks," she whispered, leaving the tent.

"Sure." He squirmed back into his sleeping bag. It was warm where she'd been. And now it smelled like her: the combination of sweat and that sweetness he couldn't identify. He breathed in deeply and thought about her narrow pale face and long golden hair. He forced his eyes closed.

He didn't even agree that they should be harbouring her. So why couldn't he stop thinking about her?

Chapter nineteen

"Happy birthday to you." Minerva woke Jacob up the next morning. "Sweet sixteen, and never been kissed."

"Put a sock in it," he groaned.

"Hey, it's not every day my kid brother turns sixteen."

To celebrate Jacob's birthday, they had a late breakfast of crisp waffles and the delicious Saskatoon berry syrup they had brought from Dora's B&B. Auntie Peggy made a special giant-sized waffle and decorated it with fruit and cream for Jacob and stuck a lit candle in the middle of it.

Everyone sang happy birthday.

"Make a wish," Sam said, "before you blow out the candle."

The first thing that popped into Jacob's head was Toby.

"Hurry up, Jay," Barney said. "Wax is dripping on the cream."

Jacob breathed in. He wished with all his might, "I hope she gets to safety." He blew on the candle and the flame went out.

"Yippee!" the boys yelled. "He gets his wish."

Auntie Peggy had three waffle machines and they were kept busy until everyone had eaten their fill.

"This must be the most delicious breakfast we've ever had," Jacob's mom said, piling up the sticky plates.

They all agreed, including Fred. "Righty-ho," he said, patting his stomach.

Jacob could see that Minerva was trying to figure out a way she could smuggle a leftover waffle or two out to Toby. That sticky syrup would drip over everything.

"Here's a birthday treat for you," Jacob's mom said, handing him a large gift bag.

He pulled out a dark blue jacket and pants. "Wow! A Jenner track suit! You know how long I've wanted one of these! Thanks, Mom."

"It's from Fred too."

"Thanks, Fred."

Barney and Sam gave him a thick book of soccer heroes and Minerva gave him a small LED flashlight that he could attach to his bike or use as a headlight.

"Thanks everyone," Jacob said, grinning at them all.

His mom said, "Sorry to break up the party, but we should leave soon if we want to have a bit of a look around Winnipeg before dropping Minerva off at the university."

"You'll want to check out the Forks," Uncle Frank said.

"What's the Forks?"

"Sort of an indoor market, down by the river. Well, two rivers, actually. It's where the Red River meets the Assiniboine. They've made a bloomin' nice park there and there are lots of good places to eat and other tourist shops."

"Oh, but you absolutely must have lunch at the Salisbury Place Restaurant," Auntie Peggy said. "It's on that new pedestrian bridge between the Forks and St. Boniface. It's a beautiful bridge, and the Sals serves the most delicious hamburgers and chips in all of Winnipeg, they say."

"What about our tents?" Barney asked.

"Leave them. You'll be back here to sleep tonight, right?"

When they were bringing their plates into the kitchen, Minerva asked her mother if she could borrow the cell phone. Jacob knew it was so Toby could call her aunt to tell her where to meet her in Winnipeg.

"But why do you want to use the cell phone?" Uncle Frank said. "We have a long distance plan and it costs just pennies to call anywhere in the country. Those cell phones are bloomin' expensive when you use them for long distance."

"Oh, okay," Minerva said. "I just wanted to-um-call the university to let them know I'm checking in today."

Jacob saw his mom's cell phone on the living-room table beside her purse. Should he take it? This might be the only chance Toby had to contact her aunt. He slipped the phone into his jeans pocket and zipped out the back door.

The Mini was parked beside the van in the short drive-way off the back lane. And standing in front of it, were Sam and Barney. They were gawking into the backseat.

"Oh no!" Jacob muttered as he hurried out to them. "Hey there, fellows," he said.

They both turned to him, their eyes huge.

"Someone's sleeping in the backseat," Barney said in a hushed voice. "Did you know that?"

Jacob peered over their shoulders and stared inside. Toby was fast asleep, curled up in Minerva's quilt. "So you found her," he said in a low voice. "You know what, guys? I have to ask you to keep a secret. Can you do that?"

"Keep a secret? Sure, I can," Barney said. "Don't know about Squirt, here though."

"Can so keep a secret." Sam bristled.

"Okay," Jacob said. "Here's the deal. That kid in there, she's got to get to Winnipeg, and it's mega-important that no one finds out about it."

"You mean we can't even tell Dad?" Barney's eyes were huge behind his glasses.

"Especially not him. He'd call the police and then they'd probably send her back home."

"She's running away from home then?" Barney asked. "Why?"

"She had to. If she didn't leave, something really terrible would happen to her. And she's got to get to her aunt's place in Winnipeg where she'll be safe."

"I still think we should tell Dad. I bet he would help."

"No. She doesn't want to take a chance that someone will call the police because they would send her right back home for sure. That's what they usually do to runaway kids. So, can I count on you not to tell anyone? No one at all?"

"Sure, I guess," Barney said. He took off his glasses and rubbed them on his T-shirt.

"And you, Sam?"

"You can count on me, Jay. I won't tell anyone. I promise. Cross my heart and hope to die."

"Just pretend you never saw her."

"Okay," Barney said. The boys shrugged and turned away to get their toothbrushes from their tent.

Jacob opened the Mini door. He had to shake Toby's shoulder to wake her.

"Here's my mom's cell phone," he told her. "Call your aunt quick because I've got to return it before my mom notices it's gone. You can tell your aunt that you'll meet her at the Forks around noon today. That's when we should be there. But keep the call short, okay?"

Toby yawned and rubbed the sleep out of her eyes. She rummaged around and found the scrap of paper with her aunt's phone number and punched in the numbers. She waited.

"There's no answer," she said.

"Try again. Maybe you dialed wrong."

Toby dialed again. "Still no answer. Wait, it says to leave a message."

"So leave a message," Jacob told her.

Toby nodded. "Auntie Charleen, it's me, Toby. I'm calling from Brandon, and we'll be in Winnipeg around noon today, so I could meet you at . . ." She looked at Jacob.

"At the Forks," he said.

"At the Forks. Sure hope you get this message. I'll try to phone you when I get there." She handed the phone back to Jacob. He turned it off.

"What if she doesn't get the message?" she said.

"She'll probably check her messages when she gets home. People usually do. Maybe she just had to go shopping or something. You can try calling her again later but you'll have to hide under that quilt now."

"You have any food? Sure am hungry."

"I think Minerva's getting you some."

Jacob managed to slip the cell phone back on the table in the living room beside his mom's purse before she noticed it was missing.

Chapter twenty

S oon after, they left on the final leg of their journey, the two hundred kilometers to Winnipeg along the broad four-lane Trans-Canada Highway.

"Not much traffic now," Jacob said. "How about letting me get behind the wheel?"

"In your dreams, buddy boy," Minerva said. "Every time you get your hands on the wheel of this baby, some disaster happens. Besides, those big transport trucks travel way too fast. This is no place for beginners."

Jacob stared gloomily at the dark green trees that covered the hills at the side of the road. "Spruce Woods Provincial

Forest," the sign announced. So many evergreen trees here, they could be back in BC.

"Guess I'll never get a chance to learn to drive then."

"Sure you will," Minerva said. "Just not here."

The trees ended abruptly and the terrain reverted to rich brown fields with rows of luxuriously green potato plants stretching out to the distant horizon. From the enormous dome of blue sky, the sun beamed down onto the highway that rippled with heat waves.

"It's so boiling with that sun beating down on the Mini roof," Jacob complained, wiping his sweaty face on his shirt-tail. "Too bad this car doesn't have air conditioning."

"Open your window wider," Minerva told him.

"Too windy for you back there?" he asked Toby when he'd wound his window down all the way and the hot breeze was blowing his dreadlocks into his face.

Toby didn't answer. She sat silently staring at the fields they were whizzing past, her long hair blowing all over the place. She pulled it to the side and started braiding it.

"You're not scared or anything, are you, Toby?" Minerva looked at her in the rear view mirror. "You'll soon be safe with your aunt, right?"

"Right," Toby said, clearing her throat. "I'll call her again once we get to Winnipeg."

Jacob thought she was trying to sound a lot braver than she felt. He flicked through the box of CDs. "How about some Bob Marley?"

"Yes," Minerva said. "Some good old Reggae to pep us up."

The first song on the CD was *No Woman, No Tears*. Jacob tapped the dashboard with a pencil, keeping time with the complicated beat. The next song was *Redemption Song*, one of Jacob's favourites. He turned up the volume so he could hear the words.

Freedom. That's what the song was about. Freedom to choose. Freedom for everyone from a life of strife and struggle. It's what his ancestors had fought for, years ago in Jamaica where they were slaves forced to work long hot days in the sugar cane fields. "*Get up!*" Bob Marley urged people now. "*Stand up for the fight.*" Jacob sang with him.

He glanced back at Toby. Running away from home was her way of standing up for the fight. It wasn't fair that she was being forced to marry some old guy. What kind of life would that be for a young kid like her? It just wasn't right.

There was a crackling on the walkie-talkie.

Jacob picked it up. "Min here, to Max."

Barney's voice came over the speaker. "So what do you call a dinosaur who sleeps all day?"

"Oh no!" Jacob groaned. "Not another one of your tired dinosaur riddles!"

"It's a dino-snore."

"And that's what you called for?"

"No. There's that excellent ice cream place Auntie Peggy told us about, up ahead a couple of kilometers. We're going to stop there to wet our whistles."

"Good plan. We're right behind you."

"Mavis's Famous Homemade Ice Cream," the sign declared. "Twenty delicious flavours."

"Back under the quilt, Toby," Minerva said. "Sorry, it's so hot. I'll try to bring you a cold drink or something."

The ice cream was creamy and sweet, and delicious, as promised. Jacob had a double scoop of mango delight, and Minerva did too. Barney had a scoop of bubblegum and a scoop of mint chocolate chip and Jacob's mom had a single scoop of orange.

Sam couldn't make up his mind. He shuffled from foot to foot and stared into the glass-fronted coolers at the enticing flavours.

Fred said, "If you can't decide, I'll have to order for you."

Sam still fidgeted, back and forth, back and forth. "Ummm," he muttered.

Finally, Fred said, "He'll have a scoop of mint chocolate chip and one of that dino-berry."

Sam was grumpy, but not for long. Once he started nibbling his ice cream he looked transported to another realm.

"Hey, Sam," Jacob said. "How come you're nibbling the ice cream, not licking it like a normal person?"

"Can't you tell I'm an Allosaurus? They don't lick. They nibble."

Minerva managed to buy a soft drink and chocolate bar for Toby and slip them to her under the quilt in the backseat.

"Blimey! I can't believe it," Fred said, leaning against the van and happily licking his large-sized double-scoop of blueberry ripple. "These six big homemade ice creams for less than ten dollars! And so deliciously rich and creamy! Bloomin' amazing!"

"See you at the Forks," Jacob's mom said to Minerva, climbing back into the van. "We'll check out the market then maybe have a nice lunch in a restaurant there."

"I don't know why we can't just get some groceries and have a picnic instead," Fred grumbled. "According to my guide book that market at the Forks is excellent."

"Now, Fred. Don't be such a skin-flint. This will be our one restaurant meal for the whole trip. It'll be our good-bye lunch for Minerva as well as a special birthday treat for Jacob. Try to keep close, Min, so you don't get lost in the city. If you lose sight of us, call us on the walkie-talkie."

When they reached the outskirts of Winnipeg, the traffic was heavy but Jacob managed to keep the van in sight while he read the map.

"There's the sign," he told Minerva. "The Forks. The van turned right just ahead."

They followed the Max into the development and found a parking spot not far from the van in a huge parking lot between two old rail cars that had been set up as candy and souvenir shops.

"Well, this is it, kiddo," Minerva said to Toby. "Here we are at the Forks in Winnipeg, finally. You okay? I'm sure there'll be public phones in that indoor market building down by the river. You can call your aunt from there."

"Sure. I guess." Toby's voice was scared. She wasn't even hiding her fear now.

"No point giving you my mom's cell phone number," Minerva said. "The only time she turns it on is when she wants to call someone. But here's Uncle Frank's number in Brandon." She gave Toby a slip of paper. "And here's some change to make the call to your aunt."

"If there's trouble, call me at Uncle Frank's," Jacob said. "We'll be back in Brandon tonight."

"You sure you'll be all right?" Minerva asked. "I don't like leaving you here when you haven't made a definite arrangement to meet your aunt."

"I'll be fine. Don't worry. Blessings and many thanks to you both." Toby's voice was stronger now. "You saved my life, you know. Truly."

"Drop us a line and let us know how you're doing," Minerva said, pulling up the hand brake. "My email address is on that paper I gave you. I'd sure like to hear from you. Stay in touch. And keep the clothes. You're a lot less conspicuous in those shorts and T-shirt than the long pink dress. In a couple of days, after I get settled in the dorms, I'll try calling your aunt's place to see if you're okay. We'll meet for lunch or something."

"So you know what to do?" Jacob asked her.

He didn't want to turn and look at the girl. He couldn't let on that someone was hiding in the backseat. Maybe Toby was right when she said, "Spies are everywhere." Anyone could be watching them.

"Yes," she said. "I'll go down to that indoor market, find a phone to call my aunt and ask her to come and pick me up."

"Will you recognize your aunt, do you think?" A worried frown crinkled Minerva's forehead.

"I'm sure I will."

"Good luck then," Jacob said. He wished he could think of something more to say to her. "Good luck," was so feeble for what he was thinking. Be safe. Stand up for your rights. Hope those creepy guys don't find you. Hope you get to your aunt's place safely. If you do see anyone at all suspicious, run fast, yell for help, hide . . . what? What could he say?

"Hey, you two," Fred called out to them. "Aren't you coming?"

"Sure." Jacob got out and closed the car door, careful not to even glance at Toby in the backseat.

"What are you waiting for then?" Fred said.

"We're coming," Minerva muttered. "We're coming."

"How about looking around that indoor market before we have lunch?" their mother asked.

"Love to," Minerva said, joining her.

"Count me out," Fred said. "I'm going to check out the river. Coming, guys?"

"We'll just take a quick look, so how about meeting over

there in front of that candy rail car in twenty minutes? You coming, Jacob?" his mom asked.

"Think I'll go look at the river with the guys," he said.

"Okay. See you at the rail car in twenty minutes or so."

Jacob followed Fred and his boys across the wide expanse of concrete and down some steps to the river.

Fred unfolded the big tourist map of Winnipeg Uncle Frank had loaned him. "This walkway follows the river to the pedestrian bridge and that famous Salisbury House Restaurant we heard so much about," he said, consulting the map.

The brown water in the river flowed by swiftly. A branch with a few leaves attached bobbed along, followed by a couple of mallards and a string of gawky ducklings.

"It's right here that the two rivers meet," Fred continued. "The mighty Red, and the Assiniboine. Sometimes in the spring, with all the melting snow and ice, there's too much water for the two rivers to handle so they get backed up and overflow their banks and this whole area floods."

They rounded the corner and a graceful bridge spanning the river appeared.

"Blimey! Now will you look at that!" Fred stopped in his tracks and gawked. "That must be one of the most beautiful bridges I have ever seen. I've read about them in engineering journals but I've never actually seen one. It's an asymmetrical stayed cable bridge. One of the most efficient and stable structures around. A bloomin' engineering marvel.

Not only beautiful, but it has a famous restaurant in the middle of it."

"Reminds me," Barney said. "Sure am hungry. When do we eat?"

"The ladies must be almost ready now," Fred said. "Let's go back up to the rail car to meet them."

As they threaded their way through the crowds, Jacob noticed a grimy beige van with darkened windows and a BC license, slowly cruising toward them. Maybe searching for a parking spot? The driver had black hair, slicked back. There was another guy inside as well, in the passenger's seat. Big guy with the broad back of a footballer.

Jacob felt a sharp stab of uneasiness.

The driver turned and stared out at him with such dark angry eyes that he jerked back. As the van slid by, he noticed a small sticker on the rear bumper. "*Repent the end . . .*" The last part of the phrase was covered with spattered mud.

He'd seen a similar phrase recently but, for a second, he couldn't remember exactly where. *Repent the end* — what?

Then it hit him like a load of bricks. Of course! *Repent the end is near!* It was spelled out with rocks near their friends' place just before they'd met Toby. Toby!

That must be her father's van! The one she'd been so worried about all along. It fit her description. Beige. BC license. Roof rack.

Maybe she'd been right the whole time. Maybe her father's van had been following them all the way from BC after all. And now, he was here, right at the Forks. About to grab her.

"Hey, Jay," Barney said. "How do you get milk from an Albertosaurus?"

"Uh . . . Don't know."

"By stealing its shopping cart."

Jacob nodded. As he followed the Finkles through the crowd back across the big parking lot toward the rail car where they were meeting his mom and Minerva, his head whirled. What should he do? What should he do? Should he say something? Maybe the guy in the van wasn't even Toby's father after all. Though he sure did look creepy.

How could he know for sure?

There must be more than one dirty beige van from BC around.

Right?

His heart pounded. Sweat ran down his back.

Chapter twenty-one

Her friends, Minerva and Jacob had gone, and now Toby was alone in the backseat of the Mini. She missed them already. Would she ever see them again? Probably not. They had turned out to be such blessedly good friends. The best.

She stared out all the windows and didn't see anything dangerous. The bright sun reflected off the shiny cars in the enormous parking lot. She couldn't shake the feeling that her father was near and that something terrible was about to happen. But there was no sign of his van.

She rolled up her dress and stuffed it into her small backpack, buckled on her sandals and climbed into the front seat. After checking the surroundings again, she swallowed hard, opened the door and slid out, reluctantly leaving the sanctuary of the little car. It had been her home for most of the past week, and she had felt protected inside.

She took a deep breath. The air outside smelled good. Fresh, and there was a hint of baked bread. Must be a bakery nearby. She was hungry, as usual. Minerva had given her a cheese sandwich earlier that day, but she had eaten that as well as the bar of chocolate a long time ago.

Come on, she muttered to herself, urging herself forward. Probably wasn't far to the market where she'd find a phone to call her aunt.

She couldn't wait to see her. It was going to be wonderful to be with her. She'd finally feel totally safe. She was sure her aunt would protect her from anyone trying to take her away. Including her father or any of the elders.

Her heart thudded as she threaded her way between the vehicles, peeking around them before crossing any expanse of pavement. There were all sorts of vans, and even a few beige ones, but none she noticed with a BC license plate.

She came to the end of the parking lot. Ahead was a huge patio in front of a large building with "Market" in big letters on it. A flash of the sun reflected off the river beyond the market building. Now all she had to do was duck into the crowd and make her way inside to a telephone, and call her aunt. And hope she would soon be here.

As she was about to cross the wide expanse of the patio, Jacob rushed to her.

"They're here! The guys who're looking for you!" he gasped. "I think I just saw their van!"

Toby's blue eyes were startled. "How do you know?"

"Beige with a BC license. And bumper sticker. Guy with black hair. Slicked back. They might be coming to get you! Now!"

"Oh no!" She bolted across the patio toward the river, side-stepping walkers and baby strollers. She searched frantically for a hiding place.

Jacob thought fast. Nowhere here to hide. And no way could he fight off two grown men himself. Especially the footballer. Fred! He had to get back to Fred!

"We got to make tracks!" he yelled at Toby. "Come this way."

She hesitated, still looking around. Then she gasped. "There they are!"

Two men approached them, their arms out to trap her.

"Tobia," the dark haired man commanded loudly. "You will come with us. Now."

"Come on!" Jacob urged her frantically. "We'll get Fred."

Toby made a clumsy lunge to secure her pack onto her back.

"Leave it!" Jacob yelled, grabbing her arm.

She dropped the pack and ran after him, zigzagging away from the men's clutches.

The men were after them in a flash. Jacob dashed away into the crowd, dodging joggers and in-line skaters. Toby was right behind him.

They ran in a wide loop around the patio. Jacob turned on the speed and pulled Toby along.

"Stop!" one of the men shouted, waving his fist. "You must stop at once!"

But Jacob and Toby kept running.

"Please, please, still be there," Jacob muttered, breathing hard. He hoped with all his might that Fred and the boys hadn't left the rail car. He couldn't think what he'd do if they'd gone.

The big footballer guy was close now. Jacob heard his gasping breath right behind him. He and Toby tried to run even faster.

Jacob spotted Fred and his boys at the rail car, looking puzzled and worried.

"Blimey! The boy can't have just disappeared," Fred's loud distinctive voice exclaimed. "Maybe he got tired and went back to the car, do you reckon?"

"Fred!" Jacob shouted. "Wait!" He pulled the panting Toby forward.

He skidded to a stop in front of him.

Fred's eyebrows shot to his hairline. "Jacob! What is it? What's wrong?"

Jacob panted. He was totally out of breath. He couldn't speak.

Chapter twenty-two

"That's Toby," Sam said, nodding solemnly. "She's our secret. I didn't tell anyone, Jacob. Really I didn't."

Jacob patted his arm. He struggled to catch his breath.

The footballer guy arrived with a skid. He was also panting hard. He lunged forward, grabbing Toby's arm and tried to drag her away.

"Let — me — go!" she grunted, struggling to escape. Her eyes were frantic.

"Toby!" Minerva called out. She arrived at a run.

"Jacob! What's this? What's happening?" his mom demanded, breathlessly. She was trailing behind Minerva.

"This child. Who is she? Where did she come from? How do you know her?"

"Hey! You let go of her!" Minerva shouted at the footballer guy.

"What's going on?" their mom asked.

"The girl's name's Toby, Mom," Minerva said quickly. "She's our friend. We've got to help her! They're forcing her to marry some nasty old man against her will!"

"Isn't she the same child we gave a ride to yesterday?" Fred asked, blinking. He looked totally mystified.

Before Minerva could answer, the older man arrived at the rail car. He was panting even louder, gasping for air. His oiled hair stood up in angry black spikes.

Toby cringed from him and struggled to pull out of the tall footballer's grasp.

"Tobia Elizabeth! You must come here at once, child!" the older man shouted. "I command you to."

"No! No!" she sobbed, breaking free from the other man. She lunged behind Jacob. He stepped forward and raised his arms to protect her as if he was in goal and about to block a sure shot. He could feel her quivering with fear behind his back.

He took a deep breath. "Toby's not going anywhere," he stated, staring hard at the man. "With you. Or anyone else. She's staying with us."

"Yes," Minerva said. "We'll make sure that she'll be safe."

"I am Tobia's father." The older man drilled Jacob with

powerful commanding eyes. "And as my daughter, she knows that she must obey me in all things. It is the holy law of God that a child must always honour and obey her father. Or she will be thrown into the Abyss and be damned forever to the Eternal Inferno," he intoned.

Jacob flinched away from the man's ranting and hypnotic stare. "No." He stood firmly, crossing his arms. "No, she won't go with you. Not when you're making her marry some old man she doesn't even know. You have no right to force her. You tell him, Fred. He can't force her, can he? It must be against the law!"

Fred shrugged at Jacob. He was still completely mystified.

"Of course he can't!" Jacob's mom stepped forward, hands on hips, face shiny with anger. She spoke directly at the man. "No child can be forced to marry anyone. This is a free country. The child is obviously frightened. No friend of my children will be forced to do any such thing." She nudged Fred. "Tell him the facts, Fred. Go ahead. Tell him now, man."

Fred shook his head and stroked his beard. "This, I do believe, is a matter for the police," he said calmly to the older man. "Meanwhile, sir, the child will remain under our protection. She is obviously distraught."

"The police? No, no. It's strictly a private family matter. Nothing whatsoever to do with the police. That child's rightful place is with us. With her family," the man insisted, reaching for Toby, with big meaty fingers. "And she will come with us immediately."

"No!" Toby squealed. She tried to push herself behind Minerva. Minerva crossed her arms and stared at the man with angry dark eyes.

"Move out of the way, girl. No spawn of the devil will prevent me from taking my own child." The man spat at Minerva's feet. "Get away from her, you filthy spawn!" he shouted, shoving Minerva roughly with his elbow against the rail car.

Her head hit the car's wooden side, and she grunted aloud in pain.

Jacob's mom rushed to her aid. "You brute!" she shouted. "How dare you hurt my child!"

"Vile devil's spawn!" The man spat in her face.

Jacob gasped and moved to protect his mom.

But Fred beat him. He flashed forward and caught the man with a karate chop to the neck.

The man grunted and swung around, his fists raised in attack. He rushed at Fred.

Fred kneed him in the stomach.

The man crouched down, groaning in pain.

Fred administered a swift punch to the jaw and the man crumpled to the ground, knocked out.

The footballer guy grabbed a piece of wood and lunged in to attack Fred.

"Behind you, Fred!" Jacob yelled, running forward. "Watch out behind you!"

Fred swung around and disarmed the big guy with a swift chop to the arm.

The guy yelped in agony, grabbing his arm. He lowered his head to butt Fred.

As the guy came at Fred, Fred shifted aside and jabbed his fingers into the guy's jugular.

The guy crumpled to the ground like a sack of laundry beside Toby's father.

"Those two will be out for a while," Fred muttered.

Jacob's mom rushed to him. "Oh, Fred. You saved us!" She hugged him tight.

"Wow!" Jacob said. "You're something else, man!"

"You're a hero, Dad. A real hero!" Barney said. "I didn't know you could do karate."

Sam hugged his dad around the waist.

"Haven't needed the moves since the Falklands when I was in the Marine .Commandos with the British Forces," Fred said quietly, stroking Sam's hair. "A long time ago."

By this time, a crowd was collecting.

"What's happening?" a young man asked.

"Those men attacked my family," Fred said. "Don't know why. Completely unprovoked. If you want to call the police to come and pick them up, that would be a good idea."

Fred gathered his family, including Toby who was glued to Minerva, and ushered them away from the crowd. "Let's go and sort out this whole matter," he said.

They found a quiet place behind the rail car.

"Fine now." Jacob's mom turned to him and Minerva. "I

want the truth from you two right now. The whole truth, and nothing but the truth."

"It's a long story, Mom." Minerva sighed wearily.

Jacob wished there was somewhere he could hide from his mom's anger.

Toby was still cringing behind him and Minerva. She looked almost as frightened of his mom and Fred as she had been of her father and his partner.

"It's really okay now, Toby," he tried to reassure her. "You'll see."

"We'll figure this out," Minerva said softly, hugging her shoulders. "My family won't let anything bad happen to you. I promise."

She tried to push Toby forward, but she was still too scared to talk. She was trembling and blinking hard, trying not to cry.

"When did you two meet this girl?" their mom asked.

"Before we left BC," Minerva said.

"BC? You mean she's been travelling with you in the Mini all that way?" Their mom's voice was shrill. "All the way from BC?"

Minerva nodded. "Hiding in the backseat under my quilt."

"I can't imagine how you managed to keep her a secret all that time."

"It was pretty hard sometimes. But even Sam kept it a secret." She patted his shoulder.

He grinned up at her proudly.

"But you should have told us," Fred said. "I thought something fishy was going on when I saw the girl alone at the side of the road yesterday."

"We couldn't take a chance and tell you," Minerva said. "If you called the police and they sent her back home, well, it would have been just so awful for her."

"I presume you have a plan?" Fred asked.

"Yes. Toby's aunt lives in Winnipeg and Toby wants to contact her so she can meet her somewhere."

"Let's go back to the van then," Jacob's mom said. "We'll call her on my cell."

Eventually, they got through to Toby's aunt. She said she lived near the Forks and she could be there at the market to pick up Toby in fifteen minutes. And she'd be wearing a red hat in case Toby had forgotten what she looked like.

While they waited in front of the market for Toby's aunt, Jacob searched the passing crowd for Toby's dad and his friend. There was no sign of them, although he did see a police car cruising by slowly. Maybe the police had picked up the two men. He hoped so.

Toby's aunt came soon. She was a big, comfortable-looking woman, wearing a wide-brimmed red sunhat as promised.

When she spotted Toby, she hurried to her with a broad smile and her arms outstretched. "I can't believe it, Toby! You're all grown up!"

Toby ran to her and they hugged for a long time. Toby dissolved into tears of relief. After her aunt gently patted her face with a tissue, Toby introduced her to the family. Then they shook hands all around, saying thank you to everyone. Jacob was last.

"I'm glad you'll be safe and won't have to worry any-more," he said, shaking her butterfly-thin hand. "Just re-member what Bob Marley says. '*You got to stand up for the fight.*'"

"I will," she said and gave him one of her brilliant smiles.

His heart lurched and he grinned back.

Minerva hugged her and told her again that she would call her at her aunt's place in a few days, as soon as she got settled in the dorms, and they could get together.

Toby's aunt thanked them. Then, after saying good-bye to Toby, and watching her being led away, Jacob's mom squeezed his shoulders and smiled at Minerva.

Relief flooded through Jacob. His mom wasn't too mad at them after all.

"I want to tell you how proud I am of you two," she said. "It looks as if you rescued that child from what I would call a fate worse than death. I do wish you could have told me about her though."

"I wanted to, but the girls wouldn't let me," he said.

Minerva said, "You can see why we couldn't."

"Yes, I understand, girl. But I'm sorry you felt you couldn't trust me."

"We wanted to tell you. We really did. But Toby kept insisting that we not tell anyone. I think she doesn't trust any adults, at all. Except maybe her aunt."

"And maybe with good reason. Do you think the poor child will be safe now that she's with her?"

"I'm sure she will be. Her aunt sounds really nice. She has five kids of her own, and they all live in a big house here in Winnipeg."

"But that man seemed mighty bent on getting his daughter back. Won't he just go there and force her to come back to BC with him?"

"I don't think so." Minerva shook her head. "Toby told me she'd heard that her aunt was living under police protection. So if Toby's dad did show up and tried to take her away, her aunt would call the police right away. I'm sure her aunt will keep her safe."

"What I'd like to know is how you managed to keep the girl a secret from us the whole time," Fred said. "And where did you actually meet her? Where did she sleep? What about food? Water?"

All the way back to the cars the questions kept coming.

"What about lunch?" Sam finally asked. "I thought we were going for lunch. I'm starving."

Jacob's mom laughed. "You're right, Sammy, my sweet. How could we forget lunch?"

"You know where I'd like to go, Mom?" Minerva said.

"Where?"

"That Jamaican café in the market. The chicken smelled dee-licious."

"Jerk chicken?" Barney asked.

"Yes, jerk chicken and black-eyed peas, Jamaican patties, pineapple-coconut smoothies," Minerva said, grinning at him.

"Fantastic!" Barney said. "What are we waiting for?"

Fred squeezed Jacob's mom's shoulders. "Good Jamaican food, here we come," he said, smiling down at her.

Jacob trailed after his family. It was amazing how the Finkles had learned to love Jamaican food almost as much as he did.

And that Fred! Man, oh man! Was he something else! Wonder if he'd teach him some of those cool karate moves. Marine commandos with the British forces in the Falklands? Wow! So that explains why he's such a kayak expert. And why he jumped right into the lake in the electrical storm and rescued Sam in no time flat.

Chapter twenty-three

After an enormously satisfying meal, the family left the Forks and drove across town to the University of Manitoba campus, Jacob keeping the Max in sight so they wouldn't get lost. He glanced into the empty backseat and sighed.

Minerva said, "Yes, I miss Toby too."

"Think we'll ever see her again?"

"I'll call her in the next couple of days. She's one brave little kid."

Jacob nodded. He stared out at the dusty buildings they were driving past and Toby's brilliant smile flashed in his head. "Mega-brave."

When they reached the campus, they stopped at the information hut where they were told how to find the student residences. They were big square apartment-looking buildings on the outskirts of the campus, surrounded by trees and lawns.

"Not bad," Jacob commented as they parked near the entrance. He bounced his soccer ball on his knee. Maybe there would be time for him to kick his ball around a bit to help get rid of that knot in his stomach.

Minerva laughed at him. "You think anywhere there's a place to kick around that ball of yours is just fine. At least give me a hand moving all my stuff first."

When Minerva checked in at the residence, her mother found out it was co-ed.

"Whatever is this world coming to?" she wondered aloud. "Boys and girls all living together? I don't know. I just don't know."

Minerva was already interested in her neighbour, a handsome, friendly young man who showed her around and helped carry her baggage to her room in the residence.

Minerva's mom issued the expected warnings. "Now, girl, I don't want to hear that you get up to any mischief in this place."

"Oh, Mom! Don't worry. Everything will be fine. I'll call you every week. Collect."

"We better get a bloomin' good long-distance plan then," Fred grumbled.

After hugs all around, Fred drove the family in the big Max away from the campus leaving Minerva and the Mini behind.

Jacob folded his arms over his soccer ball. He was in the backseat of the van between Barney and Sam.

Sam had a bunch of dinosaur figures he could bend into different positions. His purple T-Rex was attacking a yellow Triceratops, sinking its sharp teeth into its neck.

Barney was ruffling through his *Giant Dinosaur Joke Book*. "Hey, Jay," he said. "Hear about the dinosaur who put his bed in the fireplace? That's because he wanted to sleep like a log."

"Very funny," Jacob muttered.

Suddenly, he felt outnumbered. Now that his sister was gone, and his mom was Mrs. Finkle, just one Armstrong was left, and that was him.

His mom was up front, sniffing. She dabbed her eyes with a tissue.

Fred patted her knee. "It'll be good for her, Rosa. A bit of independence. Now don't you fret. Christmas is just four months away. She'll be back with us before you know it. She'll be fine. Just fine."

She sniffed again and nodded. "I know she will. She's a sensible girl. Maybe she can even bring that little girl Toby home for the holidays."

Jacob smiled to himself at that. It's true that Christmas was only a few months away.

"Now let's see if we can find a quiet road that will take us back to Brandon," Fred said.

Jacob's mom shook out the map and directed Fred out of the city to a quiet two-lane road heading west.

Barney started another one of his oldy mouldy jokes. "Hey, you guys. Did you hear the one about when an old man met a Brontosaurus coming down the road?"

"That's impossible," Sam interrupted. "Everyone knows that people weren't around when dinosaurs roamed the earth."

"I know, I know. It's just a joke. Part of my comedy routine. Okay?"

"But you should at least get your facts straight."

Jacob let out a loud sigh. Is this how the whole trip was going to be? All the way back home? He clenched his ball and stared out the side window. He wished he could be out here, jogging around one of those fields and kicking his ball back and forth, the fresh breeze blowing through his hair. He would dribble his ball on the edge of his foot, weaving it from one side of the field to the other. His toes itched and his legs twitched at the thought.

"Hey, Jay," Fred caught his eye in the rear-view mirror. "Isn't it about time you got in some bloomin' driving practice now that you're sixteen and legal to learn to drive? How about taking the wheel for a bit?"

"What? Me drive? I'd love to!"

Fred pulled the van over. He got out and Jacob clambered

from the backseat into the driver's seat. He buckled up the seat belt and when Fred was settled in the back, Jacob turned on the ignition. He checked behind. No traffic on this deserted road. He signalled and put the car in gear. He heard Minerva's voice in his head. "Ease out the clutch slowly and press down on the gas. Easy does it now."

He eased the van out onto the road as smoothly and sweetly as buttering a slice of bread. The western sky was tinged orange with the setting sun. And the road headed straight west through the golden prairie fields.

"That'll do," Fred said. "That'll do just fine."

ABOUT THE AUTHOR

Norma Charles is the author of many novels for children including *Sophie Sea to Sea*, winner of the BC Year 2000 Award, *The Accomplice*, nominated for the Sheila Egoff Award, and *All the Way to Mexico*, winner of the Chocolate Lily Award. She has travelled many times from her present home in Vancouver to Manitoba where she was born, but has never been a stowaway.

Marquis Book Printing Inc.

Québec, Canada
2008